A STREET SHAKEN BY LIGHT

ALSO BY JAMES BUCHAN

FICTION

A Parish of Rich Women

Davy Chadwick

Slide

Heart's Journey in Winter

High Latitudes: A Romance

A Good Place to Die

The Gate of Air

NON-FICTION

Jeddah: Old and New

Frozen Desire: An Enquiry into the Meaning of Money

Capital of the Mind: How Edinburgh Changed the World

Adam Smith and the Pursuit of Perfect Liberty

Days of God: The Revolution in Iran and Its Consequences

John Law: A Scottish Adventurer of the Eighteenth Century

THE FAMILY OF WILLIAM NEILSON BOOK I

A STREET SHAKEN BY LIGHT

James Buchan

MOUNTAIN LEOPARD PRESS
WELBECK · LONDON & SYDNEY

First published in Great Britain in 2022 by

Mountain Leopard Press
an imprint of
Welbeck Publishing Group
London and Sydney

www.mountainleopard.press

9 8 7 6 5 4 3 2 1

A CIP catalogue record for this book is available
from the British Library.

HB ISBN: 978-1-914495-10-6
PB ISBN: 978-1-914495-54-0
Ebook ISBN: 978-1-914495-11-3

This book is a work of fiction. Names, places, events and incidents are
either the products of the author's imagination or are used fictitiously.

Maps by Emily Faccini

Designed and typeset in Caslon by
Libanus Press, Marlborough

Printed and bound in Great Britain by
CPI Group (UK) Ltd, Croydon, CR0 4YY

FSC
www.fsc.org
MIX
Paper from
responsible sources
FSC® C171272

CONTENTS

Le soleil ni la mort ne se peuvent regarder fixement
We can no more look straight at death than at the sun

Duc de La Rochefoucauld

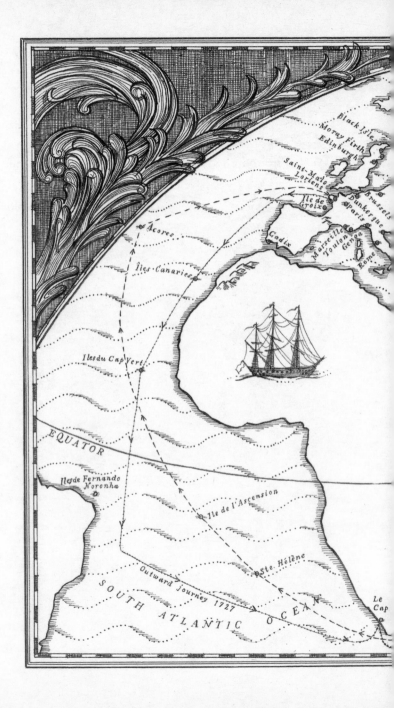

PART I

Paris, 1720

I

In the year 1720, at my age of sixteen years and some months, I went forth from the kingdom of Scotland into France. My father, who had the roup or auction-place by the Chapel in the Cowgate of Edinburgh, died that midsummer of the stone and my dear mother, appointed principal guardian and *tutrix sine qua non* by the terms of his testament, could not very well aliment both me and my younger brethren and sisters.

I had been bred for the College, and a congregation of the reformed church, but that scheme fell to ground. I had shown industry at the High School, and my tutors thought good to send me to Mr Andrew Henderson, merchant at the Schiedamse Dijk at Rotterdam, who had a side-trade finding places for Scottish boys to learn book-keeping and commercial practice in Dutch houses.

Thus wise, on the eighth day of September of that year, I boarded the flyboat *Prins Willem* at the Queensferry, with ten guinea sterling in my belt, and a bill for the same on Mr Henderson, and rolled and vomitted four days and nights to Veere, which is where we Scots have our port or staple.

Thence I went in company in a most cosie barge, drawn by horses at the side, as far as Dordrecht, or Dort as we call it, to find at the inn a letter from Mr Henderson bidding me not to come to him but make my way as best I might to Paris. Our countryman, Mr John Law of Lauriston in Edinburghshire, had erected a bank in that city and had need of trustworthy lads as commis or under-clerks. Having not funds for a horse or the diligence, I walked from Dort to Paris and saw and heard much on the road to interest me.

I learned that great King Lewis XIV had died, leaving a whole bankrupt kingdom to his infant great-grandson under the regency of his brother's son, the Duke of Orléans, a man of strong parts and excellent nature. Charmed or, some said, bewitched by Mr Law, the Duke-Regent had consented that he found a bank whose paper money-notes did much to revive the ruin'd trade of that kingdom. Mr Law then raised a joint-stock company or copartnery to trade in the East and West Indies in rivalry with the

English and Hollanders. For a while, that gentleman had been the toast of Paris and the curce of London and Amsterdam but, of late, both his bank-notes and his actions had fallen into discredit. I quickened my step so as the sooner to be at hand to assist him.

Nothing had prepared me for the sight of Paris from the Abbey of Mont-Martre. I had thought Edinburgh a great city, and so she is, but here was a continent spread below me, towers, palaces and churches all thrasted together in a reek of smoke, and through them a river that glittered in the winter sunshine. I thought that half the town might burn to ash before the other half knew of it.

There are no city walls, as at Edinburgh, but a sort of raised bank called a boulevard, where carts and coaches sailed overhead under leafless trees. I passed without hindrance through an abolished gate. It seemed the city of Paris had defeated its enemies. As I approached the New Street of the Littel Gardens, which was the address given me by Mr Henderson, I came on a tumulte of coaches and foot-passengers gathered in a mob before the courtyard gate of an old-fashioned house or, as we say at Paris, hôtel.

There was nought to be earn'd at the coach gate, so I made a scout about, and came, at the east side of the place, on a heap of debriss where a row of houses had lately been pulled down. By louping up over the rubbish, I reached the

garden wall and, sliding along as on horseback, came to
an old marronnier or chestnut-tree with a side-branch in
reach of a reckless spring. At the far end of the garden, a
serpentine line of people of all degrees and sexes shiver'd
in the sun, harassed by veteran musketeers. At the head of
the snake was one open cash-window.

I found a servants' door and came into an odorous
cellar, baled with pelts of that laborious and amiable
creature, the American beaver. The house must have been
at another time the palace of some prince or bishop,
for busts and pictures justled with sacks of coffee and other
spices, while a domed gallery was stacked from floor to
painted ceiling with the stumps of bank-note books. There
was nobody from whom to inquire the way but I could
hear the grumbling of the mob and the belling of the
Invalides, and, after many a false turn, won through to the
banking-hall. Before the open window, there was a single
cashier. Another gentleman stood at a desk, writing in
a day-book or ledger. To him I presented Mr Henderson's
letter.

The gentleman looked at me in wonder. He said that
Mr Bourgeois was not at the bank that day, and I should
return at some other time. I said that I had not come
oversea from Scotland just to go back again and that
I wished to work. The gentleman, who was named

Mr Du Tot, made a shrugg and snapped his fingers at a heap of bank-notes and a jumble of books. I was to match the note against the stump, or souche as we call it, so that I might detect and expose forgeries.

It was a humble task, but adjusted to my powers. Each note had been numbered, and cut with sheares from a book across a pattern of the initial letters JL and a lace-work or arabesque. Once I had put the books and notes in the proper progression, it was no great labour to match the number and pattern of each to each. In the way of such things, my work engrossed my faculties. After a time, I looked up and saw I was alone and the cash-window shut. I ploughed on in my apprentice furrow. My eyes began to strain and I found and lit a silver chaundelabre and did much better. In my pile of forgeries, I noted semblances that I thought could not fail to betray the character and abode of the several counterfeiters. I wrote in my Sunday French a report for Mr Du Tot and placed it on his desk.

I was thirsty, and hungry fit to relish a clagged boot.

Taking up my candle-tree, I blunder'd on a sort of kitchen and an abandoned dinner of broken baps and a jug of water. Having extended my tenemente of life, I climbed a stair with three landing-places and a balester with the same initials and lace-work as the bank-notes, but this time worked in polished iron. At the head was a gallery, and against the walls a scaffald of wooden poles and planks. The floor boards were splattered with paint and plaster-dust. I stopped before a high window. In the garden of some great place across the street, lights flickered in the trees and I heard crums of music and laughter.

"D'ye care for the view fra' here, Mr Neilson, or wad ye change it for that from atop Dunwhinnie Fell?"

I made a half-turn. Before me in the candle-light stood the handsomest man I ever saw. He was perhaps fifty years of age, tall, well-made, with on his cheek a trace of the small pox. His dress was neat and plain, and his linen and his tie of lace spotless. A full wig fell in curles to his shoulders. His eyes were of the strongest blue. He had in hand Mr Henderson's letter.

"Mr Law?"

"We shall speak in French, if you please. Would you be so good as to do me a service?"

"With pleasure, sir."

"Mr Neilson, you do not know what that service will be."

"I know that it shall be honourable and useful."

"Why, laddie, ye'll gae far and your mam will ride in a coach-and-pair doon the High Stret of Edinbro."

He led the way through the forest of poles. He said:

"Mr Pellegrini, Venetian, is painting for me an allegory of commerce. See here . . ."

I held up the lights.

". . . the Seine and Mississippi embrace beneath the winged spirit of Felicity while at the dock vessels are discharged of merchandise from Louisiane. And here . . ."

I followed him.

". . . above the door, is the portico of the Stock Exchange, where merchants in their various national costumes do business one with another." Mr Law smiled at me. "The new world will be made, Mr Neilson, if the old will budge a jot."

We came into a room beaming with light. A gentleman in a cap and gown was standing on one leg by a table covered in papers and charts. The candles in the wall-lights were of a pearly white and spread an amiable scent about the room. The lights shone off a violoncello in one corner, of deep colour and old fashion. I could tell from the resonation of my step that the 'cello was strung and tuned and that Mr Law kept the instrument in his cabinet not as trophy or item of trade, but to please a leisure hour.

"Maître Lecoq, young Mr Neilson will witness the order."

The man, who was some writer- or notarie-body, laid a

portfolio before me with a single sheet of paper. I signed under his own and Mr Law's names.

"Why, laddie, will ye not read the screed afore-hand?"

"I am here to serve you, sir, not to spy on you."

"Oh, Mr Neilson, had I ye by me these eighteen month past!"

The door yawned. There entered, in a sort of sole procession, a gentleman in his middle years, high-wigged, braided, red-faced, evil-looking. He leaned a moment on his cane, as if he were in his own house. Behind him peep'd a young lady, in dress.

Mr Law bowed. I did the same. Maister Lecoq became flat as a shadow and vanished.

"Monseigneur, you do this house an honour. May I present my confidential secretary, Mr Neilson?"

The gentleman looked through me. The young lady's glance brushed the 'cello. Mr Law saw what I saw.

"Will mademoiselle accept the violoncello as a present from the directors?"

"By no means, sir."

She walked to the end of the room and sat on a chair, out of ear-shot.

Her Court costume and coiffeor made her appear a fine lady, but she was slender, and gay as a button, and could not have been more than twelve or thirteen years of age. I surmis'd she had come from some infantine entertainment for the King at the palace of the Tuileries, a ballet or dancing-party or some tables at cards. In my life to that moment I had seen but slates and chimneys, and pigs rooting in the kennel of the High Street, and stone tenemente-lands in the rain, and red-armed wives in the Fishmarket Close, and the steading at Kerfield Mains and the arse-ends of Galloway kine and the portal of the High School and Maister Robert taking down *Durham on Death*.

Mr Law was speaking at me. "Mr Neilson, will you have the steward bring the young lady a cup of chocolate?"

I graped through the poles to the steps. As I descended, I balanced if Mr Law had private business with the angry gentleman or wished to spare me his bad manners, or both together. There was not a servant about, so I retrieved my candle, made the cordial myself, and carried it up the stair on a trey.

I heard a voice raised. The doors of Mr Law's cabinet split open and the visitor burst out, blazing like a coal. The sight of me infuriated him. He struck me with his cane. The trey flew in the air, splashing my face with hot liquor.

Through tears of rage and shame, something loomed and skimmered before me. I shook the liquid from my eyes.

The young lady stood before me, with her hand out-stretched. She said: "You are wounded, sir. Let me give you a plaster."

I took the handkerchief and put it to my scalded face. The young lady was walking away between the scaffalds. From the end of the gallery, there was a squawl but the young lady did not mend her pace. I said under breath: At the end, mademoiselle, do not turn your head. Whatever you do, mademoiselle, do not turn your head.

The young lady reached the end of the gallery and then, to cross me, turned and sought me through the scaffalds with her eyes and smiled.

Mr Law put his hand on my shoulder. "Shall we, Mr Neilson, attend to business?"

I took down four letters and copied them fair for Mr Law to sign. The church clocks sounded ten and Mr Law said he was commanded to wait on His Royal Highness. At the door, he half-turned and said:

"Have you dined, Mr Neilson?"

"Yes, sir."

"And your lodging?"

"Near hand, sir."

"Have the kindness to attend me here at seven of the morning."

"Yes, sir."

"Thank you, Mr Neilson."

I extingued the lights in Mr Law's cabinet and bunked down in an elbow-chair in an anti-chambre, where a fire still had some life in it. As I tumbled into sleep, I said aloud: "Shall I fall, mademoiselle, into your dream?"

II

Mr Law failed his appointment. At eight, I went down to the banking-hall which was empty as a sinners' kirk. I had come too late to save the bank from stopping. Through the window, I saw some working men, attended by a squadrone of archers, affixing seals to the main door. I minded to stay out of eye.

Of all places to be emprisoned for the Sabbath day, the hôtel of the Royal Bank and Company of the Indies at Paris was not the least convenient. I found some dried fruits of Persia, and coffee of Moka, and sugar from the isles, and wine of Shiraz, and made a good breakfast. Believing that I should make myself useful to the King's receivers, I enterprised a budget or inventoire of the active in the house: a very littel silver coin, a great many letters of exchange, stock in trade, spices, Indian cloths, furs, pictures, busts, printing-irons, books and looking-glasses.

I had never in my life been so happy and never more so than when, walking the length of Signor Pellegrini's gallery, I saw, in the plaster-dust, the print of mademoiselle's little wee shoe. As for the handkerchief, it was embrodered with a coronet and a coat of arms, formed of a silver cup on a black field. Surely, there could not be so very many families in France with such an achievement. I found a lavandrie and washed my linen to be ready for business on the morrow.

I was standing within the main door at seven of the Monday morning when I heard the seals being broke. The receveurs were five in number. They jumped.

"Gentlemen, I have drawn up a preliminary statement of assets."

"And you, sir, are?"

"Will. Neilson, Scottish, underclerk."

They took my inventoire and made their way to Mr Law's cabinet.

An hour later, I was summoned from my bank-note pudding. The gentlemen were seated behind the great table, as in a tribunal or session.

"Mr Neilson, would you confirm that that is your sign-manual?"

It was Maister Lecoq's order.

"That is my signature, gentlemen."

"Please wait on our pleasure. You are not to leave the Bank."

"I have no wish to leave the Bank, gentlemen."

Another hour passed, and I was called to the main door. There stood an officer of the King, Mr Duval, and a troop of archers. I was commanded to be the King's guest at his Castle of the Bastille. I asked Mr Duval why I, a second-commis and a foreigner at that, had been selected for so signal an honour, which words caused Mr Duval to laugh heartily and slap me on the back.

As we passed through town, he repeated my words at each crossing and provoked the coach-passengers to lower their glasses and laugh and even bless me. We passed a handsome square, called the Royal Place, and approached the eastern boulevard, where stood a tall, old-fashioned fortress, bristling with towers, joined by a high curtain wall with atop it a gallery of wood. Beyond it was a ditch with a burn choked with rubbish, animal skins and flapping corbies, and beyond that gardens, pleasances, deal-yards, stables and farms. The eastern breeze blew cald across the fields.

At a postern gate, kind Mr Duval took his leave and I was taken into a yard with a row of poor shops. The shops were shut, and the soldiers of the guard masked, which lowered my spirits a rung. A bell rang out in dismal welcome. We crossed a little bridge into a courtyard, with on the left or north a second drawbrig into the castle proper, and on the right side, beneath an old mulberry tree, a dwelling-house.

In the house, I was received by Mr Maisonrouge, the governor of the castle. He said that, so long as I should be the King's guest, I would receive a pension for my diet of a crown. If my friends wished to supplement His Majesty's bounty, they were free to do so. I might call for my furniture, but no writing tools nor paper. If I had other requirements, I had but to request them. His civility emboldened me to say that, newly arrived in France, I was eager to study her constitution and wished he might furnish me with an almanack of the ancient and noble families of the kingdom, with their arms and devices. As with everybody that memorable day, he started, as if the buttons on my coat were so many fire-arms.

"In the fulness of time, young gentleman," he said. He rose and left the chamber.

I was blindfolded and taken, with many a trip and stumble, over what sounded like a wooden bridge and then across a paved or cobbled court. We came inside and climbed a turnpike stair to the fourth landing. I was pushed forward and my blindfold untied. Then, with a grinding of locks and shooting of bolts, the door closed behind me.

I found myself in a large room, with dirty walls, scribbled with charcoal marks, two cold stones to support a fire, and the end of a tallow candle in a brace on the wall. Light came from three splayed loop-holes, and also that biting east wind. From nearby came the sound of some machine. A grabat of straw, without bed-clothes, and a sort of gardy-roby supplied my elemental needs.

"O Mam, if you could see your elder now!"

I sat down on the hearth-stone.

After a while, I stood up and started to read the messages on the walls but they dejected me. Husbands missed their wives. Mothers missed their children. One cursed, another praised, His Majesty. While I was so engaged, the door ground open and a troop of men stepped in, carrying dishes, firewood, a table, linen and a chair. In a moment, the hearth was ablaze and the table laid, and I was seated before my dinner, with a ragoût and a roast fowl, a species of bread that was soft and white as a summer cloud, and a bottle of Burgundy wine. As I feasted, the men sprang like Jack-in-boxes to serve and pour. To my pleasanteries they gave no answer.

When all was cleared away, including table and chair, the men returned. It seemed they required their pots of wine.

"I shall reward you for your service just so soon as His Majesty's Treasury has released my pension."

There was a general scowl.

"Meanwhile, in a day or two, my friends will hear of my plight and send assistance. You have heard, no doubt, of the famous Mr Law?"

A man spat on the floor.

"He has fled the Kingdom . . ."

". . . else he'd be strapped to the wheel in the place de Grève, and I'd have first strike with the hammer."

"My friends, you are quite mistaken."

They spitted and spat, stamped feet, turned backs and left the room.

III

The castle of the Bastille at Paris is a peaceful place. For a building so extensive, it is quiet and I quickly learned to distinguish sounds: the bell of the Cathedral of Our Lady, the cry of the gateman admitting carts through the Porte Saint-Antoine on the north side and the grummelling of a mill, which my warder told me was the powder-fabrick at the Arsenal to the south. In the evening, there was a marching and drumming in the court below, as the keys to our chambers were handed to the King's Lieutenant, Mr Maisonrouge.

As to my entertainment, I saw no more tablecloth or Burgundy wine, but had a crock of bouillon, a piece sour bread, and a jug of excellent water. I was confined my chamber, except at noon, where a warden took me up the turnpike stair so I might exercise on the top of the tower. The cold blue lift caused my head to swim.

I looked down upon an open space, triangular in form, which must once have been a defensive bastion that projected from the city wall. It was now appropriated to a kail-yard or potager, about which circumambulated a half-a-dozen men, whom I took to be my fellow guests. My eyes were drawn to a gentleman in full pereuyk, braided coat of crammasy velvet and long lace cuffs, who walked with difficulty, supported by several youths in livery.

The next day being rainy, the bastion was deserted. As I made my hundred paces atop the tower, I was joined by the well-dressed gentleman, with but two attendants. As we passed for the second time, I said:

"May I present myself, sir? Will. Neilson, Scottish, underclerk at the Royal Bank of Paris."

"Ah," he cried, falling back on his supporters. "Another dupe of Mr Law!"

"Sir, I was not duped by Mr Law nor by any man. I hold it to have been the honour of my life to have served that gentleman, even for a short time. Good day to you, sir."

He arrested me with one hand. "Kindly leave us," he said and the young men stepped away. "You will learn, Mr Neilson, that it never harms to take some care in this place. I, too, shared in Mr Law's counsels."

"And your name, sir, if you will permit me to inquire it?"

"Bigby, captain of vessel, and commander of the Company's port at L'Orient in the States of Brittany."

"Have you news of the gentleman, sir?"

"The hand-letters had him stabbed by a creditor in the street at Brussels. Yet, today, I read he has been seen at the court of the Archbishop-Elector of Cologne. My belief, Mr Neilson, is that he will join the Royal Family at Rome. You will know that His Majesty has had no secretary-of-state since the defection of the Duke of Mar."

The Jacobite blutter flew over my head. None the less, I had known in my own kin Jack and Whig a-coodle in the marriage-bed. Why not a prison oversea?

"Have courage, Mr Neilson. Mr Law shall return and reward his friends. Anselme!"

One of the young men stepped forward.

"What are the primes on offer in the Street today against Mr Law's return to the Kingdom?"

"I can lay twelves, Captain."

"There, Mr Neilson, you have it. Neither likely nor impossible."

IV

I had no duties and no occupation. I thought of every scrap of beef or mutton I had ever tasted, of the kitchen fire at Grandfather's farm or the August sun on the flank of Culter Fell. I piled up Bastilles of wind and sleet, snapping with pennons, and handed mademoiselle over the antick threshold.

"Mr Crotte, I need a chair."

"A chair he wants, my friends. What, may I ask, is wrong with the King's floor?"

"The chair is not for me."

The turnkey paled and walked out arseward. A little later, my door opened, and a broken tabouret skeltered across the floor. I performed on it some reparations.

Once I had a chair for her, she came at once.

"Will you not yourself sit down, Mr Neilson?"

"I shall never sit in your presence, mademoiselle. Also, I have no second chair."

She sat down and ordered her skirts.

"Will you tell me your name, mademoiselle?"

"Alas! I do not know it. I am the daughter of a noble-man who does not like to lose money. I believe my mother is no longer alive, else she would have escorted me back from the Tuileries. I have a funny wee face and rich brown hair and the daintiest foot you ever saw. My bosoms are small, but that is because I am just twelve or thirteen years of age. Next year, when I am thirteen or fourteen years old, I shall have a more womanlier shape. Is it true, Mr Neilson, that in portions of your country, the civil government is deputed to goblins?"

"It is true, mademoiselle."

"Singular. Do you like music, Mr Neilson?"

"Yes, mademoiselle."

"I play a great number of musical instruments but cannot, at present, say which ones. I have a gift given me by God and were it not for my elevated rank, which sets an embargo on public performance, I would be the first of the musicians of France. Will you kindly light your fire, Mr Neilson? I am very cold."

"I have no fuel, mademoiselle, and if I burn your chair, you shall have nowhere to sit. May I take you in my arms and hold you, mademoiselle, and then we shall both be less cold?"

"No."

"Why not?"

"Because I am the greatest heiress of France and you are a Scottish gentleman, imprisoned under sealed letters in the Castle of the Bastille. Also, my father, whose name I do not know but whose blazon is *Sable, ane cover'd chalise argent*, has shown no preference for you, but rather the contrair."

"What if I achieved glory in the service of France?"

"Then I think he might look with favour on you. But, Mr Neilson, you must act soon. In four or five years, I shall be married, and then you shall have lost your chance. Mr Neilson, forgive me, I cannot stand this cold."

"Will you come again, mademoiselle?"

"I shall come whenever you call me. I beg you, Mr Neilson, for your own sake, to make this place less cold."

"Mr Crotte?"

"Does Her Ladyship require a sopha?"

"Not at all. Rather, mice and other small deer run over my face anights, interrupt my slumber, and make me surly in my dealings with you and your compagnionrie."

"They are the King's mice."

"Then summon the King's cat, you wretch!"

The light was fading when the door sounded again, and

something scritched through the air, hit the wall, made a subbersalt and landed like a feather with feet. It sat on its hanches, glanced at me without interest, and proceeded to make itself presentable.

"You are right welcome, Puss."

The animal took no notice. After a while, it made a saunter of inspection and then returned to its place and toilette.

I woke in a furnace. On my chest, Mistress Puss was currying her paws. Small creatures the size and colour of molds burrowed into my armpits, three and three. I sat up with my passengers. I said:

"Well done, Puss. I believe you shall be an admirable mother."

She took the compliment as her due. Every now and then, she rendered a low growl or burr to call one or other to the bath. That night there was a slaughter of mice, the more terrible for being altogether silent. At sundown on the next day, having purged my apartment, Puss waited for the door to open.

The turnkey threw a kick. Madame Puss sprang onto the flying shin, hip, chest, shoulder and through the door, while one lagging foot ploughed three cramoise furrows in the man's cheek. In the morning, the mainoeuvre was repeated in reverse, so that the poor man had, at the least, a symmetrie of wounds. The next evening, he held the door for her, and Puss, like an armed duchess, processed out.

My duties, in her absence, were not burdensome. She had initiated her kits in the mysteries of the garderobe. Our preferred game was as thus: I would herde my charges into a corner and, with threats and oaths, vow their immediate extinction. They trembled in a mewing ball, begging for quarter; and then, by some secret signal, sprang under, over, round and through me, and collected in the far corner, where the action was refought. Then they fell asleep on my chest. I thought: By this age of life, Alexander of Macedon had won a pitched battle.

V

I had been in the castle some ten or fifteen days when my turnkey brought in a suit of cloths, a bukket of water and a razour. I was to go to my interrogatory. I was led, without blindfold, across the court and into a second, and up a broad worn stair into a council room. This time, there were three gentleman, seated before a table spread with an Italian carpet. In the middle was a young man, scarcely older than I, flanked by two others, one tall, one small. The small gentleman's chair was set at a skew, as if he were not wholly committed to the proceeding. It was only when I began to speak that he looked at me with a curiosity like a blade. On the table-carpet was the portafolio and the famous order.

The young man spoke. "Mr Neilson, would you confirm that that is your sign-manual?"

"You should be aware, gentlemen, that the conditions of my lodging are making me worthless as a witness. Would you kindly order the window-shutters closed?"

When that was done, I glanced at the order.

"That is my signature, gentlemen."

"Did you know what you were signing?"

"Gentlemen, I am a sub-clerk of the Royal Bank and Company of the Indies, and not one of its directors. If I recollect, it was an order to transfer 250,000 silver piastres from the Company's agent at Genoa to the order of His Eminence Bishop Belsunce in Marseille to relieve the poor of that town stricken by plague."

"There is no plague in the Kingdom of France."

"Well, shall we say epidemic distemper?"

The little gentleman barked.

The young man looked at me. "Mr Neilson, you should

know that the debtors of the Company of the Indies are now the King's debtors. Since Mr Law, to my anger and regret, has absconded the Kingdom, you are now liable in person to the King for the sum of one million livres tournois. Where is that sum?"

"Not here, sir. As you can see."

"I have the power, Mr Neilson, to put you to the question."

"Remind me, sir, if you will be so kind, what question you wish answered."

There was another bark. I was of a sudden weary of the Kingdom of France.

I said: "I fear, gentlemen, that Mr Law has given you a false impression of Scotch civility. You had better kill me under torture for, if you do not, I shall kill you, and burn your houses, both at Paris and on your lands, disgrace your wives, geld your sons, ravish your daughters.

"But wait! I have run away with myself. His Royal Highness does not love you. He loves Mr Law. When that sagacious gentleman returns into the sunshine of His Royal Highness' favour, he will say, after an hour: 'Where is my pet nevoy, Mr Neilson, in whom I have the highest hopes?' And you will say, 'Alas, monseigneur, he killed himself in despair in the Bastille of Saint-Antoine,' and Mr Law will not believe you."

I stood up. "I now wish to return to my apartment. I have a family of cats there who depend on me for their provision."

VI

I forgot to say that, by attaching myself one day to Mr Bigby's troops, I had stepped upon the bastion, and the guards, thinking that I was now admitted to its liberties, allowed me there with my escort. On the morrow of my interview, I was taking the air, when I saw Mr Bigby coming in the opposite direction, supported on two footmen.

"Good day, Captain Bigby."

"Ah, my pet nevoy, Mr Neilson, in whom I have the highest hopes!"

Bombaz'd, I continued. On the next circuit, Mr Bigby stutter'd:

"His Royal Highness does not love you. He does love Mr Law. Ha-ha. Very good, Mr Neilson."

"May I ask, Mr Bigby, how you have the process-verbal of my interview of yesterday?"

"It is in the news-letters. Run, Gidéon, bring them from my apartments." One of the laddies detached himself in a sulk.

The report, which covered a double sheet of in-quarto, was precise to the word.

"There was no secretary I saw. Unless some spy was listening through the wall . . ."

"Who were the gentlemen, Mr Neilson?"

"They did not favour me with their names. There was a young talking man, and then one of the middle age who had some knowledge of the business of banking, and a third who said nothing but laughed."

"The young man was Mr Argenson, lieutenant-general of the police of Paris. The second, I'd wager, was Mr Pelletier, controller-general of the His Majesty's finances. As to the third . . ."

"He was a small man, who regarded the others with contempt, and seemed tickled by my answers."

"Of course! M. le duc de Saint-Simon, His Royal Highness' friend and, I should add, an admirer of Mr Law. He records everything said in his hearing. Bravo, my lad!"

"So I am not to be tortured."

"Of course not. The virtue of the French, which is also their vice, is levity. To be ridiculous in France is one thing, to be spiteful and ridiculous another. Will you not dine with me tomorrow to celebrate the auspicious birth of the Prince of Wales?"

"Alas! I am confined for all but one hour each day to my chamber."

"I shall care for that."

As I descended with Mr Crotte, I was met by a gust of heat and the savour of roasting meat. The door was opened on an apartment the quadruple of mine, with a window in glass. Before a wood fire, a busy man in a leather apron was turning whole fowls on a spit. On the chimney-breast hung a full-length portrait of a naval gentleman leaning on a table with charts and a spy-glass, and in the background men fleeing in boats from a burning warship.

The hero was seated in a high chair, while comelie lads stood at their ease or swung their heels on damask-clad armchairs. Ladies was there none. What caught my eye, on the groaning table, was a pitcher of milk.

"Dear boy, welcome. Will you not join us in the loyal toast?"

"I would lief, Captain Bigby, just beg that drap o'milk to carry away to my lodging."

"Come now. You shall have both milk and Champagne."

From one of the laddies I received a brimming glass of wine.

"Now, gentlemen, I give you the King!"

"The King!" I cried.

"But which King, Mr Neilson?"

"The King of Scotland, England and Ireland!"

"He at Rome, Mr Neilson, or the chap in Hanover?"

"Both, Mr Bigby. All of them. Wherever they are. Gentlemen, I give you the Kings!"

There was a roar and a smashing of Venetian glass. I had never before tasted Champagne. I wondered what Providence had composed such nectar for poor men.

"Ha-ha. Very good, Mr Neilson."

The master-roaster had his hand on his hip.

"Let us dine, gentlemen."

One of the young men sat more close to me than I am used to. I moved away.

"I see, Mr Neilson, that ye have yet to taste the sweets of Sodom."

"Captain Bigby, I have yet to sojourn in any Biblical city, but I assure you that when I do none of you shall hear of it. I do not despair of one day winning the heart of a fair and virtuous lady."

"Bah! Women are all pox't. I'll have nothing to do with 'em. And yet," he said, laying his head to the side, "one hears whisper of a great female, who is curious whether your firmness of character is matched in your corporal constitution."

There was a cackle from the boys.

My face was hotter than the hearth. I mummelled: "I know no such person."

Captain Bigby had served with valour in the English Royal Navy. At the Revolution, he had been cashiered, though whether for attachment to King James or some peccadille, I could not discern. King William had given him leave to find his bread where he might, and he had enlisted in the French Marine and commanded the *Fortuné* of sixty-four guns at Toulon. He had met Mr Law at Genoa in '12 or '13, and later at Paris, and been charged by him to erect a port for the Company at L'Orient on the Atlantic coast. In the summer just past, ill-intentioned persons, envious of his success, had conspired against him. Arrested without a jot of evidence on a charge of dilapidation, he had been ordered to the Castle, but the Duke-Regent had been kind enough to allow him his men-servants, whom he called his mignons or pets. The Captain's principal occupation, as far as I could descry, was stock-jobbing. Every now and then, a lad would arrive with prices from the rue Quincampoix, which is the Mercat Cross or 'Change Alley of Paris.

I escaped with my jug of milk.

VII

The first consequence of my celebrity was rather disagreable than not. The lady fishmongers of Les Halles, touched by the plight of my pets, convened for their relief. Rather than select each day some tid-bit for Puss to apportion as she felt just, each sent her basket of leavings, which arrived in my cell at noon in a steaming mound of heads, backbones, tails, gills, fins and guts. Puss would not touch the disgustful fare.

The stench penetrated every corner of the castle. Mr Bigby, who hated all things unclean and wicked-smelling, shunned me on the Bastion while one of the mignons made a remark so unkind to the feminine half of Creation that I gave him a buffet and the Captain had to separate us.

I feared Puss might leave me. Amid the stench, Mr Maisonrouge caught the whiff of sedition. The King's Crier was sent to the market cross, which gentleman in a thunderous voice commended the ladies for their zeal in His Majesty's service, but ordered that no further fish remains, whether scaled or unscaled, be sent to the Castle of the Bastille, on pain of an amend of ten livres on the first offence, and, on a repeat offence, one week's detention at the Hospital of the Salpêtrière. There were no more baskets and in time the stink lifted.

The second consequence was that I received an order on the King's Treasury, signed by that most clement prince, the Duke of Orléans, that I was to have an allowance of ten sols a day for the maintenance of my dependants. I had firewood, and milk, and bread, and felt myself to be lapped in superfluity. The third consequence was that, amid offers of engagement and a proposal of marriage from a cat-fancying lady of Cambrai, I received a book. I knew before I unwrapped it that it had come from mademoiselle.

It was a Latin Bible in-folio.

I had but reached the Book of Amos when a second packet arrived. It was the works of Horace, printed at Milan in the year 1472, and bound in recent times in intolerable splendour. Within the front board, the bookplate had been cut out. In my fancy, I thought mademoiselle was dipping her father's book-presses and taking the first volume she could reach at. A week later, I opened Machiavel's *Discorsi* on Livy, printed by Aldus at Venice *anno* 1540. It was full of diminutives, as if Signor Machiavello had learned his Latin from a Corstophin mamie. Yet as I hirpled along, I found a strong mind and a clear expression, and began to think for the first time about the purposes of political government. Then no more books came. I hoped that mademoiselle had left a kindly interval so that I might master the vulgar tongue. Nothing came and I douted that the fair felon (as I thought of her) had been caught red-hand and the libraries placed out of bounds.

My courage came back to me. I was certain that Mr Law would return to France and employ me. While he spun his visions of prosperity, I would attend to particulars, and we could not fail to put France back on her feet. I had no doubt that Mr Law would reward me and I would buy title to some lands that conveyed a county or marquisate, and parade before that angry man in a coach-and-six. I would set my dear mother at ease, furnish joyntours for my sisters, and educat my brothers at schools and trades as their tutors should think most convenient. I would then place myself in the hands of mademoiselle, to devise for me a deceint and valuable path of life.

My entertainment varied with the chances or hazards of Mr Law's return into His Royal Highness' favour. If, perchance, there was in my bouillon a crum of pig fat, then I knew that the odds that day in Quincampoix Street had shortened. My belly was as perfect a stock market as could be. Mr Bigby's gazettes had Mr Law at Venice, living from play. I wished him to stay in good health, for if he died, then so should I.

I had baptised the kits with the names of the minor prophets. One day I found that Zephaniah, a brindled tom of broad intelligence, was missing. I searched every cranny of the cell. Puss was unruffled. The next day we were down to four kits, and then to three, and then to none at all. I understood that now her bairns were grown, Puss was sending them out to win their livings in the mousing trade, where the Castle of the Bastille offered field for advancement. I said to Puss that, if she were dull, and had a mind to take a second husband, I would be pleased to accommodate them and any progeny God granted them. Puss demurred, not, I believe, because she feared a second tom might bide out late and fall into scrapes, but because she wished to preserve the memory of her lord who had given her such brave and industrious kits. We were acquaintances, perhaps, more than friends.

VIII

The days elapsed, running into each other like winter streams. Each day was a little worse than the day before, and then very much worse. I was never all awake, nor ever all asleep, but roamed a kingdom of phantasms and shy desires. My hearing was so sharp that I thought to detect, one morning from the gate, a woman's bare-foot step on the causey. Another day, I heard the groan of a creel being set down and again lifted. From those scraps I made a world. I walked five leagues round my walls each day, sometimes to the tip of Broad Law, sometimes along the haughs from Peebles to Innerleithen, once carrying mademoiselle over a bog so that her stockings should not be wetted.

At Advent of 1723, I learned that the Duke of Orléans of glorious memory had died in the arms of the young duchess of Fallary or, as Mr Bigby said with his Sabbath-day sneer, his regular confessor. My hopes fell away. There was now no chance that Mr Law would return, or that I might make name and fortune before mademoiselle's nubility. My pension, already many months in arrears, ceased altogether. I cannot now remember how Puss and I won through that winter of '23, but we did.

My dishevelment disgusted Mr Bigby as much as my pruderie bored him. A coldness fell upon our intercourse. What puzzl'd me was that the Captain, though an adherent of the disgraced Mr Law, continued to live in good cheer. His troops, if anything, augmented. Not that he neglected me. He was kind enough to send sometimes a worn justicoat, or a broken pair of shoes, not worth the turnkeys' taking for themselves, but welcome enough to me.

I jelous'd that the Kingdom of France had forgotten me. Mr Argenson was no longer lieutenant-general of police. Why should they release me? The King was paying my diet and since it came not to me, it must have passed to others for some useful or pleasant purpose. Yet I did not regret my insolence at the interrogatory, for though it likely had cost me my life, it had adverteised my place of detention to mademoiselle. If I survived in a cranny of her heart, then that was well enough.

One night I woke and Puss was seated on my belly. Before her was the warm body of a brown rat.

"It will come to that, dear friend, but it is not now."

My mind was like an open moor, with thoughts like blirts of rain or sparks of lightning. I lost my scruple about my dear mother. I cut two pages from mademoiselle's Bible, found a corbie's quill on the bastion, and fashioned lamp-black and spittle into ink. I wrote to my mother under cover to Mr Warpoll, His Britannic Majesty's Ambassador at Paris, sealed it with tallow, and gave it to Mr Bigby. He called one of the mignons to take it to the post-house. I waited and I waited until the thing fell through the sieve of my mind.

I knew I had been forgotten, and that would be my escape. One day, the turnkey would not lock me in, or I should be left at sundown on the bastion, and I would find my way out and nobody be the wiser. Then another notion burst in my mind like a grenade, and levelled the castle.

"Are you married, mademoiselle?"

"I believe I am, sir, though I cannot say to whom. I believe something else has happened to me, else I would have sent you succour in your distress. Will you not, to flatter me, Mr Neilson, shave your beard a little and cut your hair?"

"I have no money for the barber, and Mr Maisonrouge will not allow me razor or sizzars lest I end my life. Will you judge worse of me, mademoiselle, if I do end my life? I think of that all the time. Strange to say, it is what keeps me alive."

"I most certainly shall, Mr Neilson. Do I, just because I have not married the Scottish gentleman who caught my eye, do I trip about killing myself? I would have you show a little firmity. Fie, Mr Neilson! I think worse of you already."

"There will come a time, mademoiselle, when I can bear this existence no longer."

"It is not yet, Mr Neilson. You have Madame Cat for your provision, and you have just to call me and I shall come."

"I will have to burn your chair."

"Then I shall stand."

49

IX

In the year 1725 or 1726, the Company of the Indies passed out of the King's domain and back to its shareholders. In the gazettes and hand-letters, which Captain Bigby received in profusion each day and read with care, there was printed the Company's repaired balance. The bank-notes, which had collected in the rue Quincampoix like slop in a stable-yard guttar, were written off as wholly without worth. Among the bad and doubtful debtors was M. Neilson, Scottish, whose liability of 1,218,994 livres and 8 sols at the 25th penny shall be added to capital as and when it is recovered. Now that I was a debtor not of the King, but of the actioners of the Company of the Indies, I felt my prospects were a little less drear.

One morning Puss did not return. She, who with another had kept me alive, had left me. I riddled my brains to find if I had offended her. Then I bethought me that Puss, like many feminines of the different species under heaven, would rather leave too early than be left too late. At mid-morning, I received a note from Mr Maisonrouge saying that His Majesty no longer required me, and I might expect to leave the castle before Michaelmas.

On the bastion, I carried my news to Captain Bigby. His face dropped.

"O, dear boy, how I shall miss you."

"Captain Bigby, it shall be my first care once at liberty to petition for your immediate enlargement."

He looked away. "Shall you wait upon your benefactress?"

"Who, sir?"

"The great lady who interests herself for you."

"If you mean my dear cat Puss, no. She left me yester-eve. I have no other patroness."

"Let us walk a little."

I steadied him with my arm.

"You should understand, Mr Neilson, that not everybody in France saw, as well as you and I, the solidity and elegance of Mr Law's system. There are persons outside this house, ignorant persons of all degrees but with no grasp of the finances or of commerce and navigation, who bear a resentment against him and his friends. It is better, for the moment, that I remain under the protection of His Majesty. He has been gracious enough to allow me diet, my books, my cellar and my servants and, at times, to send to me for elucidation on certain matters of long-distance trade."

"I see."

"I have no family but my sister in Lancashire, and she is provided for."

"I see."

"You shall not forget me in the world, shall you, Mr Neilson?"

"Never, sir."

As the month of my release approached, I regained my novelty. Mr Maisonrouge had me to dine. I received a most courteous letter from the Directors of the India Company, engaging me as a sub-clerk or writer at Chandernagore on the River Ganges in Bengale, with appointments of 2,000 livres per annum, such monies to be held in trust in France until my debt to the Company shall have been discharged. I calculated that, even at simple interest at the 25th penny, or as we say four *per centum*, I could not pay the debt before Judgment Day. At compound interest, Eternity would not suffice. His Majesty was gracious enough to provide me with a suit of clothes and twenty livres as journey-money to the Company's port at L'Orient, on the Atlantic coast of Brittany. It was with exaltation that I set out, by the Saint-Honoré gate, feeling the sun on my back and the use of the legs that God had given me.

My stroll across France took three weeks. I was distressed to see, in the States of Brittany, mile after mile of unculti-vated land. In Low Brittany, which makes a sort of rinn or paeninsula, everything of a sudden became little: round

hills and wee fields hemmed by live-hedges and hogged
oaks, sunken roads and straggle villages where none but
the curate knew French or could show the way.

Lorient itself, which stood on the north shore of a
broad estuary or firth, was a place of stops and starts.
Founded by Mr Colbert in the great King's reign, it had
fallen into decay until taken over by Mr Law in the year
'19. At his disgrace, it had again lost its friends. It was now,
I was told, to be revived not only for the rigging of vessels
to the Indies and China, but for ship-building, repairs
and carinage, and as a market for their merchandises.

At the port, which occupied a front of about one
thousand toises along the river Scorf, there was but debris,
a rotten slip-way and, on a little hill, a pair of wind-mills,
a bakery for galettes or ship's biscuits and, beyond it,
an idle powder-factory. Beside a rope-walk on the land
side was a little town drowned in mire.

For all my oeconomy, I had not funds enough for the
Golden Lion inn and lodged with a private hostess,
Mme Julie, a handsome widow-lady somewhat between
two ages. She gave me a room at the second-pair front,
with a corner window overlooking the muddy firth, where
I could see my ship, the *Prince-de-Conty*, at anchor in the
rode being made ready or, as we say here, armed.

Mme Julie thought me skinny. At the ordinary each

day at noon, she stood over my chair till I had finished her fricassay and drunk her wine. She made me cast my linen after just a day's wearing, and was for ever pinching my fore-arms, or brushing dust from my shoulders, or testing the buttons on my coat, or lifting a smut from my eye, or tieing the latchets on my boots. From a lady less comelie, such attentions would have been vexing.

I had looked forward to giving news of Mr Bigby to his friends. I was deceived. My fellow-boarders bickered to extol his profligacy. I heard that he was conveyed about his domain in a launch manned by twelve sailors in gallooned green cloth with gold braid and velvet buttons, each livery costing two hundred crowns. Ships swung on the anchors for fourteen months while their crews sickened and cargoes spoiled. Oak gun-carriages rotted on the quay for want of a ten-sol tarpallion. The Germans and Switzers engaged to work Mr Law's plantation in Louisiane starved in their scores at Ploemeur. Nobody inquir'd of my opinion. When for all that I gave it, and said I found Mr Bigby a good man and a good servant of His Majesty, they looked at me a moment and then returned to their yarn. It seemed to me that, in damning Mr Bigby, they were preparing for their own failure.

My days I passed in martial exercises or at the hôtel of the Company of the Indies, reading the edicts on our

trade and informing myself about the empire of the
Grand Moghol and the factories of the French, Dutch,
Portuguese and English. Men in town talked of Malabar
and Pondicherry as if they were no more distant than
Quimper. In reality, there was but one book that interested
me and that I never missed to take down. It was a history
of the Peerages of France from the earliest times to the
accession of Lewis the Great.

Her name is Joyeuse.

The dukes of Joyeuse, now in their ninth descent,
possessed lands throughout the Kingdom. I dared not
search out mademoiselle lest I embarrass her before father
or husband, and miss my sailing. Mme Julie chuttered me
for my silences.

I wrote a letter to the Fauxbourg Saint-Germain, which
is the district of Paris for people of condition. I said that
William Neilson, Scottish gentleman, was now at liberty,
and bound for the service of the Company of the Indies
in Bengale, where he should be absent many years; and
that his dearest wish before he sailed was to thank Mlle
de Joyeuse for her charity. If she were to write a line to
him at the hôtel of the Company at Paris, saying that she
was in good health, she would relieve a troubled heart.

In my walks along the frith, where all the winds of the
Atlantic fought to cut and bite me, the letter had many

variants. While to myself that version reeked with passion, a husband or father could, I thought, find no solid ground for jealousy or suspicion. I hovered about the post-office and made the plunge.

I received no answer.

I woke to a cannon shot, and then two more. Through the pane, I could see the pavilion of the *Prince-de-Conty* at half-mast.

I jumped up, crying, "Mme Julie! We are sailing."

She ran to the window in her apron, turned and sprang at me.

"Next year, you go to the Indies. This year, you stay with me."

All her clucking and scolding was gone. Mme Julie stood on the boards with her heart in her hands. It had not occurred to me that a second woman might like me.

"Oh sweet madame, forgive me, but my heart is given."

"She is not here, Mr William. I am here."

I was filled with sadness. A tear rolled down her cheek and splashed on the boards. She turned and said: "I shall pack your portemanteau."

On the quay, you never saw such scenes of grief. The sailors stood in daze, while wives and daughters water'd them with tears and kisses. Mme Julie handed me my bag,

retied my tie, brushed my coat, shook my hand. As I
mounted the launch, a lackey in the Company's livery
pushed through and handed me a letter. It was from Mr
Ambassador Walpole at Paris, and enclosed another from
cousin John Melvil, which last said my dear mother had
died and been laid in Greyfriars Burial Yard, on the
brae-face, by Sir John Murray's tomb. I leaned on the rail
and I confess I wept. I wept for my darling mother and
for my sad hostess on the quay, for Mr Law and Captain
Bigby and for Puss, for the fair land of France receding
from me, and for its fairest inhabitant.

PART 2

———⟡———

Voyage to the île de France, 1727

———⟡———

X

At the île de Groix, where we loaded cannon-powder and waited on our wind, there was a commotion beneath the bow. A priest of the Roman church stood upright in a launch, bellowing in English:

"Take care of my packteels, you devils."

Breathless at the top of the sea-ladder, the divine lighted on me. "Do you speak Our Lord's English, young gentleman?"

I stood up. "I do, reverend father. I am a Scotsman of Edinburgh. Will. Neilson is at your service, father."

"A heretic and a whigamore, I would punt."

"Both, father, but with a slight proficiency in the English language."

The ecclesiastic's cargo, consisting of about two dozen wooden cases, was stakked on the fore-deck, while the subrecargue, as that officer is known, measured and calculated. He explained to me the infringement. I translated into English.

"Your pacotille, reverend father, is nearly twice the volume permitted by the Company of the Indies. Mr Saint-Martin insists that you return half the cases to your launch."

"What you see here is the fruit of the vine of the Champagne. To the hot Christian gentlemen of Pondicherry, it is as the rivers of Babylon."

I turned to the Company officers. I said: "I have no stock-in-trade, gentlemen. Please write the half of the reverend father's goods to my name."

"God will not for ever leave you in darkness, my son."

The reverend gentleman's name was Father Patrick O'Crean, younger of an old family of Galway in the west of Ireland, late of the seminary at Nantes and bound for a chaplaincy at Pondicherry. Captain Butler de Saint-Paul, himself of Hibernian stock but bred at Saint-Malo, had engaged him as almoner of the vessel. We were placed together beneath the dunette or quarter-deck, in a small cabin made all the smaller by the reverend father's stock-in-trade. I had to scale over the boxes to reach my cot. Our door opened directly on the Great Chamber, which might have been great could one stand in it or squeeze between a dining-table and chairs and four 24-pound cannons. Two ladies and their husbands shared our elevated accommodations, while the bachelor or celibatory men were bunkered on the middle deck in the Saint-Barbara, the lair of the master-gunner and his cartridges, where also were the quarters of the surgeon-major and purser.

At five of the clock on March 4, 1727, the wind blowing from the north-east, in a piping of whistles, grinding of the cabestan and a final cannon shot, we were under way.

The *Prince-de-Conty*, vessel of five hundred tons gross and one hundred and forty-five crewmen, was a city. Leaving the reverend father to his prayers, I found the main deck encumbered with stock-in-trade, chests, barrels, surly sailors and charcoal for a species of still to make seawater potable. As for beasts, it was a marine steading with chickens in cages, sparrows and canary-birds, rabbits, geese and ducks, while on the deck below were pens of beeves, veals, two milk cows, pigs, sowes and sheep, and hay and grain to entertain them. There were old men, young men and little boys. I could not turn about without knocking off a hat. For a day, I watched the coast of Brittany pass by at two or three leagues each hour.

Where the wind was at our stern, it caused a horrid

rolling. Father O'Crean kept to his bed, exhausted by sea-sickness. Tending to him helped me forget my own queasieness. On the fourth day, we doubled Cape Finisterre in a squall of rain. A great wave ran over the deck taking a dozen fowl-cages with it. A poor dog that was howland with fear died in my arms.

It became warmer. The sailors worked in their shirts while even the passengers had gained what we call their sailor-legs. On the seventh, we saw before us the isle of Palma, with Teneriffe to our babord or left, its peak girdled with mist and flashing with lightning. I saw fish that flew over the waves as far as a flushed pairtrig, and schools of tunny that followed us for days. We hauled up shoals of a creature the sailors called a bonite, somewhat like our mackerel and just as greedy, for I had but to throw out my line to feel a pull on each hook. The sailors filled pails of the creatures to feed the pigs, but I begged a dozen to salt in the Scotch fashion as a whet for my suffering friend on fast days. I had learned in the pools of Tweed to swim like an otter but as I lay to sleep I knew here was but twelve inches of Béarnais oak between me and my reward.

The sailors did not seem to me quite of the world. Those who worked aloft called to one another two hundred feet above as if in their own parishes. They spoke with indifference of kings and princes but obeyed the piping command of a boy officer. Each man mistreated the man below him, always with interest, and the poor mousses or cabin-boys worst of all. In their smudged faces, I saw an invincible resolution: that, one day, God would give them someone yet lower to bully. Each day at noon, I watched as Captain Butler and the master-pilot estimated our height or latitude with an instrument called a nonante.

Though a passenger at the table, as we call it, Father Patrick preferred to keep his room. I sensed that my reverend friend was made shy by his defective, or rather, non-existent French.

He seemed to descry my thought for he said: "At the seminary, all instruction and devotion was in Latin so I never had the occasion to employ the French tongue. What needs a man, young William?"

"Faith? Grace? Good works?"

"All is vanity, young William. What needs a man but a bottle of Champagne for his breakfast and a shining guinea for his Phyllis, without pinching for three or four day afterward?"

"*Nescias an te generum beati*
Phyllidis flavae decorent parentes . . ."

"Yes. Yes, and that."

"Will you expound something to me, Father Patrick? I

had heard that the priesthood of your church was bound to the celibate life."

"That shows, if evidence were needed, how little a heretic such as you knows of religion. You are correct in so far that marriage is not permitted the higher clergy. Informal, mercenary, temporary or otherwise irregular liaisons with the feminine laity, while not literally enjoined, are none the less not proscribed."

"Ah. I did not know that, Father Patrick."

"Else, you understand, the clergy would become dishevelled and unwell and could not do God's work on earth."

On the twentieth day we felt the Alizé or trade winds from the north-east. The sailors strung a canopy from fore to aft to protect us from the heat. The planks of the deck scorched my feet through my shoes. The sailors worked barefoot. Towards nightfall, we saw a steaming peak called the Isle of Fire. We were bearing towards the islands of cap Verd where we were to take on cattle and water.

As we approached the isle of Santiago du cap Verd, there was rather shouting and confusion, but our first pilot, Mr Quérel, pursued his own way and we anchored at fifty fathoms in the mouth of a desert bay. On the land, there were two wells. One, the nearer to the shore, had been spoiled by two Dutcher vessels lately come in. A second, some two hundred paces further on, was clearer but it was a labour to bring up the water from the depth and carry it by a chain of men to the boat. Seeing me at work with the sailors and marines, Captain Butler ordered me back to ship with some asperity.

I whiled away the hours by inquiring into theology.

"The Trinity?"

"Yes, the Trinity, father."

"It is the great mystery of our faith. Let me explain in a species of parable. Make a fist of that strong right hand of yours."

I did so.

"Now. This finger, your first finger . . ."

He unbent it.

". . . is Jesus, our Saviour."

"And this, your middle finger which I straighten now in all humility and hope of salvation is Mary, his blessed mother. And this, your ring finger is . . . Remind me of the name of Our Lord's father?"

"God?"

"No. The other one."

"Joseph."

"This one is Joseph. You have it. Jesus. Mary. Joseph. The blessed Trinity."

Father Patrick leaned back. He was moved to the

marrow of his being. "It is more profound than that, William, inestimably more profound. Yet that is sufficient for you at this point in your formation. The errors of Calvin recede. I shall make a good Catholic of you before I am done, and a Tory."

"Thank you, Father Patrick."

XI

On the Sunday last before Easter, which was the thirty-fourth day of our campaign, Captain Butler sent to me to inquire if Father O'Crean would be well enough to celebrate Mass on the holy-day. I was instructed to reply in the affirmative. When the day dawned bright and clear, and the men began to congregate on the main deck, I found my religious friend still in bed.

"I do not feel especially well this morning, William. I believe you have reached that stage in your preparation where you may take divine service unaided. Not the full Mass or sacrament, of course, for you are not ordained. You may celebrate some of the lesser rites. You shall wear my surplis which is somewhere at hand."

"It is knotted about your head, father."

Every Scotsman loves to preach. I selected for my text Proverbs 23:31: "Look thou not upon the wine when it is red, when it giveth his colour in the cup, when it moveth itself aright." I put in as many saints, devils and angels as I dared. I was glad to hear my voice amid the rigging and see the sailors' upturned faces below me. Captain Butler was kind enough to say that he had found some edification in my discourse.

I returned to find my chum still in his cot, with a bottle well down below the waist.

"Father Patrick, I do not presume to intermeddle in your work, but you will have no stock to sell at Pondicheri."

I had heard that in the Indies men would pay for each bottle of Champagne a pistole.

"Consider the beasts of the field, William, how they live. They toil not, neither do they do very much beside. I have with me something of far greater price than the wine of the Champagne."

"The Holy Gospel?"

"Like the Holy Gospel."

The Roman church became my calling. Captain Butler, who approved the influence of religion on the equipage, allowed me his Bible and missal and I read morning and evening prayer and the litanies of the Saint Virgin at nightfall. On Sundays and feast-days, I spoke Vespers from the deck so that the men might hear without leaving their mainoevre. For the Captain's table, I composed a Grace in far-flung Latin so that my faults of doctrine might pass over the bowed heads. Each Sunday, I instructed some thirty or forty mousses and novices in the lights of the Roman, Catholick and Apostolick religion, one of the older lads interpreting (or so I trusted) into the Armorican or Low Bretonne tongue. No longer a passenger, who is a personage of no consequence on ship-board, I had become in some degree a part of Captain Butler's staff or état-major.

I accompanied the ship's surgeon, Mr Saoule, to attend those daily injuries and sicknesses that are the lot of the poor sailor of the open sea. I crept along the lower decks where some poor fellow was shaking with fever in a sack of sail-cloth of six feet by two feet above a lake of sheep's piss. I thus came to know, as far as it is possible for a land's man, the disposition of an armed merchant vessel of the French marine. Though I was accustomed to close living from the tenemente-lands of Edinburgh, those odorous Babels were no preparation for the stink of the lower decks of the *Prince-de-Conty*. Mr Saoule said the stinkier the better for us, for that meant that the water in the cale had long sat there.

I learned from the sailors to watch and listen and feel. The savour of the wind, the colour and taste of the sea-water, a pelican that landed on the deck that they caught with their hands: all were *empirica* that might preserve our lives. At night, while the passengers rattled cards and bottles, chess-men and dames in the Great Chamber, I read to Father Patrick from the Bible, translating as best I might from the Latin. He found Our Lord's Passion distressing, and thus I selected milder themes, such as the Book of Ruth, the Drunkenness of Noah, Balaam's Ass and Samuel's prentissage with old Eli, which became his favourite.

"When I ponder your conversion, William," he said, "I ask myself: Why was this task appointed me, the weakest of Our Lord's servants?"

Father O'Crean's reputation for sanctity, far from suffering from his occultation, augmented by the day. Captain Butler had straw laid outside our chamber-door, muffled the bells that called the watches, had the boatswain abate his loud-hailer or *porte-voix* and sent each day to inquire after his almoner's recovery. Father Patrick alone was permitted a light in the night-watches. While even the commissioned officers had one lean day in two, my friend had beef bouillon twice a day, prepared by me at the Captain's hearth, and fresh bread from the baker in place of biscuit. The ladies encumbered me with cordials and muffs to take in to the patient. My own diffidence in matters of Gallican doctrine cast a brilliant side-light on his learning. Mr Butler was kind enough to say that I was doing quite well, for a young man, in hard circumstances.

One still morning, Captain Butler summoned me to the dunette, a sacred space or temenos to which only his favoured officers might step. Leaning over the rail, so that his words flew down into our wake, he gave me instructions that I found cloudy and hard to discern. I sought Father Patrick's advice.

"Of course you should attend to the new converts and supply the lacunae in their knowledge. Yet, young friend, I would have you proceed more in gentlenes than in hard and sharp words that might bruise their simple souls."

"I believe, reverend father, that Captain Butler suspicions there are Protestants a-board."

"Protestants! God forbid that there should be any such upon this sanctified vessel. I mean, apart from you, young William, but each day your errors scatter on the bosom of the ocean."

"Thank you, Father. I believe Mr Butler suspects there may be secret conventicles between decks."

"Leave them to their errors, young William. What man among you, having ane hundred sheep, if he loses one of them, does not rejoice in the ninety-nine that remaineth him?"

"Captain Butler thought to hear psalms."

"Psalms, you say. That cannot go. Have an ear always for psalms."

The sailors' religion was like to that of the Greeks. The sea and the ship were scenes of ghousty war, where every spar or engine had its ambushed imp or custodial saint. They called on Saint Pump and Lady Cabestan and cursed the devils gambolling in the shrouds. Yet though, in the night watches, I listened out for psalms, I heard not a snatch.

That Sunday, I took as text for my exhortation the seventeenth verse of the eighteenth chapter of the Gospel of Saint Matthew: "And if he will not hear the church, let him be to thee as the heathen and publican." At the close, Mr Butler looked at me in secret understanding as a thief his pal at the Fair.

XII

The *Prince-de-Conty* was as hot as a forge. There was not a breath of wind, no dawn and no dusk. I searched in vain for the pole star. At night, flying fish tumbled into the sails and fell to suffocate on the decks. There was no need to cast a line. Harassed in the water by bonites and by fregate birds in the air, they seemed the most unlucky of creatures.

"Do not seek to know God's purposes, young William," Father Patrick said when I had dressed the fish for his dinner. "Be sure only that all the works of nature, how alarming so ever, combine for the prosperity of God's creation."

All night, the sky flashed with lightning. By day, blirts of rain, which we call grains, soaked the main deck. The sailors were wet as water-spaniels, while I delighted to bathe for an hour on the dunette in the falling rain. The ship was ringed by sharkes or sea-dogs, swimming with ease and in whole silence. Each was attended by other fish, one called a pilot and another a sucet, like parasites and flatterers about a great man. In return for certain servile offices too scandalous to recount here, they received some scraps from the magnate's table.

We were drifting back from the Line of the Equator, as if Leviathan had her nose against the prow.

XIII

On the forty-eighth day of our voyage, we at last doubled the Line and passed into the Southern Sea. At noon, Captain Butler and Mr Quérel, the master-pilot, took our latitude with the nonante. When Mr Quérel turned, and announced that we were full twenty-minutes south, there was a roar from the decks and rigging.

The maître, coming to the foot of the dunette, bowed to the Captain and then to me, and begged to know if there were any candidates for Baptism. Baffled, but taking my direction from Captain Butler, I said there were. All those for whom this was the first crossing of the Equator were formed into a line on the foredeck, while sailors armed with every species of pot and kettle massed in the spars and shrouds. We processed the whole distance of the deck, and assembled on the fore-gaillard.

I was determined that the Baptism, which was no sacrament but a sort of antique Saturnalia, in which the violent subordination of life about ship was reversed, should in no way trespass on the reverend father's dignity. Captain Butler shrugged. It seemed there was no choice in the matter.

The ship fell silent. From the main hatch, there appeared a singular figure. On his head was a chaplet of parrel beads, which fell to his feet. His beard and hair were of spliced tow. Three strands of cable made his belt while a harpoon did duty for Neptune's trident. A second figure, covered entirely in a robe of tarred hemp, set up a desk of planks across two barrels and, with all the pettifoggery of a bedel or kirkmaster, laid out his ink-horn and paper and a gamell or mess-tin for our offerings.

Neptune turned a magnificent eye on me and asked if our vessel, which had never crossed the Line, should be baptised. If not, he said, she should be doomed always to sail within the Tropicks. I gave my assent. We then made a second procession round the deck.

On the fore-deck, at the foot of the misaine, a great bukket of three feet in depth and four across, covered in tow, was filled with sea-water. Across it was one of the barres or handspikes used to turn the cabestan. Two sailors, their faces horribly blackened with pitch, held each end of the barre. Each candidate to be sauced, as they called it, was seated on the barre, then immersed, while water rained down from the sailors in the riggings.

The bedel had begged, or taken, from Mr Quérel a sea-chart and each candidate for baptism was given the name of a place of that geography. One of the lady passengers, who was well-shaped, was christened Bay of Heats. She took it in good part, giving a crown to be spared the saucing. Mr Pinasse, a first-lieutenant who was not liked, was Isle of Rats. Mr Rivouay, the writer or purser, who was careless of his linen, was Stinkards' Bay.

Having no money or strong waters to pay my ransom, I was baptised twice, once for myself (as Orphans' Bank, which is a fishing-ground in the mouth of the Saint-Laurent) and once for my suffering friend as the Bay of Angels, in the government of Savoy. There followed a water fight in which I planted my standard before the hind-mast or artimon. My scholars rallied to it and, though outnumbered, we were by no means disgraced. At the end, which came more from lassitude than any order from the officers, the offerings were counted and they amounted to twenty-one piastres and as many cups of eau-de-vie. When I recounted the bicker to Father Patrick, he was much delighted.

I told him how, in the most brilliant passage of arms, Joanick Tareau, my usher or nomenclator, who as I said knew some French, crying "Care for my parents!", swept up two kettles and plunged into the mass of the enemy at the foot of the main mast.

"Did you reinforce such reckless bravery?"

"I did, Father Patrick, though I gave no order. The whole troop followed in their hero's furrow. In the shock of our descent, the enemy fell back and we gained command of the main pump."

"The pump! The pump!"

"Then, with half our strength giving cover, the other half worked the wheel and sent a jet of bilge water across the deck, forcing the enemy back to the fore-gaillard.

Even Neptune and the beadle took to flight. But our triumph was short-lived. Our hero fell, brained by a mess-bowl. Without their champion, the lads lost heart and I ordered a general withdrawing to the artimon. There, with but seven others, and those wounded, we waited for the end. The lads, who knew their times had come, distributed their few possessions in charity."

"Fortunes of war, young William. Had I been there, we might have prevailed for Mother Church and the Royal Family. None the less, you have lit a flame that will resound down the ages."

"Yet, reverend father, though in command of the field, our enemies hesitated. I think they feared that our dwindled force might still have teeth to snap. From the gaillard came a herald at the beat of the drum, with an offering of a bottle, and a demand for a Holy Truce so each side might collect its wounded. My officers were for refusing so shameful a convention but I . . ."

"Correct! William, you read the signs of the times."

". . . seeing our champion stir from his inconscience and stupor, demanded the bottle be placed beside him."

"Blessed are the peacemakers for they shall inherit great riches."

XIV

For many days and nights, we sailed by the bowline or close to the wind. Our second sow farrowed twelve grice. The sailors, soppie and good-hearted souls, reserved for the dam scraps from their mess-bowls. The night sky was so changed I felt light-headed. I gawped for hours on end at the Southern Cross.

On the sixtieth day, the sailors felt the winds from the north-west that would carry us round the Cape of Good Hope. Great birds, in form like a gull but the size of a grey goose, which the sailors called sea-sheep, were a sure sign we were in its vicinity. The weather was delicious. We began preparations for doubling the Cape. The sailors brought up new cables for the rudder and the riggings, and put up reserve sails on all the masts, lashed the three boats, and attached two axes to the artimon in case it had to be cut. On the morrow, the sea was covered in mist. At noon, a wind sprang up, and before we could take down sail, we were shaking like a fever patient. Seas ran over the deck while, in the Great Chamber, four windows smash'd though their shutters were barr'd with saltires. Water pour'd under the door of our cabin as from a sluice. The cords holding the chests of Champagne parted and only with all my strength was I able to hold them secure.

The wind abated. The sun appeared. Coming on deck, I found a knot of officers about our master-pilot. The lead had touch'd bottom at seventy-two fathoms. A little later, a sailor called land from the main mast. It astonished me that Mr Quérel, the master-pilot, after sixty-five days sailing and two thousand leagues, without a sight of land since Santiago du cap Verd and every sort of storm and calm, had brought us to where, exactly, we needed to be. Captain Butler ordered that we put in at the Dutch settlement to make reparations.

The Hollanders' rode or anchorage lay below a broad mountain called Table Mountain, as flat as an altar and covered with a white mist falling in fringes like its linen cloth. Beneath it was a white town seeming to have been made from playing cards. All about us sea calves and pingouins splashed and pranced as if delighted at our arrival. After the sailors had dropped anchor, I led the company in the *Te Deum*. I counted fourteen Dutch vessels in the road.

Captain Butler sent instructions that while the carpenters and caulkers worked on the vessel, all the sick should be taken ashore to profit from land air and fresh vittal. I was commanded to attend Father O'Crean and, if that should be possible, take him out of town into a farm or wine-garden, where he might enjoy healthful exercise. The officers left in the long-boat in good humour.

My friend joined me at the rail. "So, young William, shall we not find us four merry mevrouws to make our hearts glad in Ashkelon?"

"Alas, reverend father, I have given mine away for all time and I could not attend to the happiness of even a single of your beauties."

"So. Only two ladies?" He looked heart-broken.

"If you would be so kind, reverend father."

I suffered much feminine teasing that evening amid trailing vines but it dissolved in Father Patrick O'Crean's good nature. In the wine garden, which lay three good leagues by cart the thither side of the Table Mountain, Father O'Crean seemed to know what was what.

At midnight, under barbarian stars, I set out with the overseer's son to climb the Table Mountain. By a sort of reversal, the firm ground made me wamble and totter. At first, there was a serviceable path but, as the world began to light, we entered a steep ravine scattered with boulders and sand, with damp places full of sweet-smelling herbs. After toiling for some three hours, we reached the table. The sun was rising to the east, whitening the mountains to each side. To my left, as on a map, I could see the Cape and False Bay and the mountain called the Lion. Beneath me was the town, the star-fort and the Company garden laid out like an embroidered napeking. Out in the rode

was Robin Island and the *Prince-de-Conty* no bigger than
a nut-shell. Beyond was limitless sea. A troop of the apes
called bavians wished to share our breakfast. When my
companion thew a stone to disperse them, they answered
with a salve of missiles and a peal of insults and injures.
As we scuttled for cover, I thought: What an Eden God
has given us for our habitation! On the way down, we
boiled in our skins from exertion and the sun.

We foregathered on board as if after a festival. The sick
appeared much restored from being on land, and the lady
passengers thought to see a better colour in our clerical
patient. Captain Butler embarked cattle, sheep and all
sorts of good vegetables, and for some time we made
good cheer.

XV

From the Cape there are two principal passages to the
Indies. The northern passage is by the Canal of Mosam-
bique and the top of the Isle of Madagascar. The Directors
wished to experiment a southern route, a deep bow to
latitudes thirty-six or -seven degrees south, the better
to catch the wind. We were headed, I was informed, for

a relâche or landing on an island Mr Law had colonised
and named île de France. The Dutch India Company had
settled the isle, but could do nothing with it and, having
a more convenient station at the Cape, had abandoned
it some twenty years before.

Up to now, I had been concerned only with mastering
the clerical profession and fulfilling, as far as I was able,
those ghostly duties that Father Patrick was prevented
from absolving by his very delicate state of health. In the
way of such things, I became, in my daily round, more
aware of the navigation. I could see that it was not wholly
happy. The petty officers among themselves spoke only
the Armorican or Low Bretonne tongue. I had heard that
it had some congruencies with the speech of our Scotch
Highland men, which my grandfather spoke with ease,
but I could detect none. I did remark in the men certain
attitudes and gestures, as if they were on the top of
questioning an order. In part, I thought that a resentment
natural to those raised in the bottle, as we say, towards
officers who have learned their craft from algebra and
quadratick equations.

On the eighty-first day, Joanic Tareau fell to his death.
We had a fresh wind from the beam, and to reef the
hune-sail the lad had clambered up the shrouds on the
tribord side. The ratling parted under him and he tumbled,

head-first, to the main deck. The crew was distraught, while Captain Butler said, in my hearing, that the lad was the most promising mariner for his age he had ever commanded. Attended by his school-mates, I read the burial service while the company snevelled. Joanic was sewn into sail-hemp and two thirty-sixes tied about his feet. They proved inadequate, for as he fell astern down the tribord side, he became engulfed in the turbulency made by the rudder, where he stayed for all to see for a good four hours. I never heard such oaths which abated not at all in my hearing. When I inquired from Mr Rivouay, the writer, the names of the poor boy's parents, so that I might write to them from Bengale in feeble consolation, he opened the rolle and said that the lad had none. I wished to be alone with my tears, but there is no place to be alone on a French merchantman in the Indian Ocean.

Then, on the hundredth day by my journal, a sailor was given the calle for smoking behind the main mast whilst on faction. He was lowered from the mizaine spar and dunked in the sea. He was dragged in our furrow until, at a signal from the master-at-arms, he was pulled up more dead than alive where he thraw on the deck like a dying sharke. The men sulked. I became vigilant, prepared at a moment to report to Father Patrick any hint of contumacie.

XVI

I seemed to be tumbling in a barrel. I was being dragged in a barrel behind a cart. The sound of the wheels on the pavement deafened me. I woke to a roar. Our silly cabin was shaking.

Outside, the wheel was spinning without a man to tend it. Through the door was an unvarying whiteness of sky and foam. The main deck and forward gaillard were a mass of people, weeping and crying and fighting with one another. The sails were torn to ribbons and could not be reefed or furled. On the babord side, I could see, at a distance of two cable-lengths, a gash of white where the waves were breaking on some rocks or fringing reef. The crew had thrown out four anchors at the bow and two beyond the stern. The force of the wind was lifting the bow as if the *Prince-de-Conty* wanted to sit down on her rump. In the tumult of impressions, I thought: Why so much sail abroad in such a tempest? Why did the master-pilot come so hard by a lee-shore? I shouted for order, but the wind in the rigging drowned out my cry.

I ran back to our chamber. Throwing open the door, I was intoxicated by fumes of wine. The Champagne cases had split, and bottles were tumbling and smashing in the bilges.

I said, as mildly as I might: "The vessel is in difficulties, father. Will you kindly rise and partially dress?"

Father Patrick O'Crean rose in his night-shirt. There was a jolt which threw me against the partition. The ship sprang back, like a horse bitten by a snake. One of the fore-cables must have parted.

"Kindly wait for me on deck, my William. I shall not be long."

The wind in the rigging made such a howl that one could not make oneself heard. I struck the bell, over and over, to call up the men to the upper deck, but it made no sound above the din. The captain and officers were nowhere to be seen. In the struggle for the boats, all distinction of rank and sex had vanished. I shouted against the wind: "There is nothing we can do in this shambles. Come, father. I am a strong swimmer and the shore is no more than a gun-shot distant. Hold on to my belt."

I turned. Father Patrick had on his cassock and over it his surplice and stole. In his hand was the *porte-burette* which contained the vessels for the Holy Supper. He shouted close into my ear:

"How can I leave these poor people without the succour of religion? For you, William, the fruit of my life, there is another task. Take this thing, polish it, and give it to the King, my master."

He thrust a leather pocket round my neck.

"Father, I shall attend you."

He pressed his hand against my chest. I lost my footing, tumbled against the rail and then was falling through warm water white as snow.

As I rose up into pandemonium, I saw Father Patrick, upright on the poop deck, his crucifix raised to Heaven, the sailors on their knees about him, clutching at his gown. I heard through the wind the phrases: *Salve Regina, Ave maris stella*. Then the bow cables parted, the vessel spun like a dog chasing its tail and with a sound that it is still with me, the main mast broke at the base and rolled over the deck taking my friends with it. The vessel shivered and came down on her beam-ends.

I dived down through the spouts of water, again and again, hoping to see my brave friend's black cassock or any man who might be saved.

I feared I would have no more strength and, in tears, I turned for the shore. The water was whipped into peaks like cream. I thought now only of myself.

I could find no passage through the reefs. Each time I approached, a wave picked me up and threw me against the sharp rock. My clothes and skin were torn and my head rang from the blows. I was losing my strength. Pushing out, I let myself be dragged down along shore in the hope that a fresh-water burn or river had made a break in the reef. I thought: I, who swam Tweed at Berwick on New Year's Day, and who wished to save my friends, cannot even save myself.

Above me stood a black man as naked as the day he was born. He bent and with a sweep of his right arm pulled me up and over the reef.

PART 3

Port-Louis, 1727

XVII

Dawn found me under cover. I was lying on the soft floor of an open cave. A green fire was burning, and the African gentleman was attending something in it. He saw me, smiled, and passed me something in his hand.

It was so hot from the fire that I dropped it. It was some fruit or vegetable, cooked in the fire, fibrous, both sweet and not sweet, and most welcome to me.

"Do you speak French, sir?"

"Yes."

"May I inquire the name of my saviour?"

"François Delacour."

"May I thank you from my heart, M. Delacour?"

"Do not thank me. I saw the ship break and a boy cutting the waves like the dolphin who will take the burden of this life from me."

Mr Delacour doused the fire and covered it with red soil. I guessed, without his telling me, that he was a runaway slave. The storm had stilled and all around was steaming greenery. He led the way through the woods. To me they seemed impenetrable, but he knew paths where I saw only great rocks, fairns and lianes. Sometimes, we came on little camps, with boughs laid for a bed, where one of his fellow maroons had passed the night. Sometimes, my companion would growl, and another black man would appear at his elbow. We crossed numberless burns brought down to a trickle, and fallen boughs covered in paddock-stools the size of futballs. Parrots darted about us.

At camp that night, Mr Delacour said: "When we become tired, we go to the Rock. After a time, M. Morpath sends soldiers along the shore and we jump into the sea."

"Fie, M. Delacour! Self-slaughter is the greatest sin. Let us go to your Rock, and fortify it, and invite M. Morpath to leave us in peace. We shall have freedom, and laws and justice, and religion, and God will smile on our commonwealth."

"God does not know us. A French man stands each side of the gate of Heaven with a drawn sword so none of our people may come in."

"M. Delacour, that is not the case. Heaven is open to

all Christians whatever their nations. And if my sins shall be forgiven, I shall plead your cause at the Throne's foot."

He looked up over my shoulder. "I am weary, Mr Will. I want to go home."

The next morning, we came after two hours in sight of a high bare rock, shaped somewhat like a giant's thumb. From just beneath the summit, I looked down on a village, with a single street scattered about with wooden houses, a harbour with a half-built earth and timber fort, irregular fields fenced with dead thorns, and a sea without shipping.

"What is this wretched place, M. Delacour?"

"Port-Louis."

"Give me your hand, M. Delacour."

As we stumbled down the makeshift road, black men and women in the fields straightened, dropped their tools, and ran to the fences. There was a whistle and then another and, before us, were European men, freckled or burned red by the sun, their hair like barley-straw. I was knocked to the ground. When I picked myself up, I saw Mr Delacour, with a sort of collar round his neck, being dragged downhill and on his face a far yon look. One of the Europeans turned, raised his piece, laughed, and fired above my head.

I stood up. A little above the village, to the left of the harbour, was a house which, though built of wood, was more straight and better-made than the others. I jealoused that to be the seat of what passed for government in this forlorn station. By the time I reached its portico, I was as wet with sweat as if I had come direct out of the sea. An Indian gentleman, whom I imagined to be the maître d'hôtel, blocked my passage.

"I have urgent business with M. Morpath."

"M. le marquis de Maurepas is not receiving."

"Are you sure, sir?"

I plunged past him into a room, open on all sides, where men lounged in elbow-chairs in their shirts. My own extreme negligé was hardly out of place.

"M. le marquis?"

"Who seeks him?"

"Neilson, Scottish, writer at the Company's factory at Chandernagore. It is my dreadful duty, sir, to report that the Company vessel, the *Prince-de-Conty*, Captain Butler commanding, was wrecked on the île d'Ambre last Tuesday morn."

"Do you think I do not know that, boy?"

"I can guide a team of men to the place."

"There were no survivors. Except," and here he stood up, "except you. Now why is it that of all the worthless men on the vessel, the Devil selected Mr Neilson for salvation?"

There was horrid laughter.

"M. Delacour, an escaped slave, plucked me from the sea when all my strength was gone. I beg you, Excellency, to preserve his life and I myself shall work to make good his master's loss."

There was another laughing. Mr Maurepas raised his hand for silence.

"What do you know of Major O'Crean?"

"I knew him only as . . ."

I bit my lip.

". . . a good and brave man who gave his life for his ship-mates."

"That is as may be. He was also a secret agent of the Pretender, and was carrying something of value to Bengale. Did he have cargo with him?"

"He had Champagne wine, though it had a little spoiled in passage."

"I mean gold or silver, boy, or jewels."

His eagerness disgusted me.

"Refused. Get out."

As I shuffled through the warm house, the maître d'hôtel overtook me in a fuss. I thought to hear him say: "Go to Jaan Begum. She will help you."

Out in the sunlight, a young lady, in a dress of yellow silk, was being helped by an officer into a carriage. I had not ever imagined a carriage in Port-Louis. Two other ladies, also in dress, stood in attendance. Across the yellow lady's shoulders was a Cachemire shawl. To that I addressed myself.

"I have a favour to ask of Mme la marquise."

She did not turn. She was struggling to bring her panier within the carriage-door. The officer let go of the pleats of her skirt and placed his right hand on his sword.

"I am, madame, the only survivor of the wreck of the *Prince-de-Conty*. A runaway slave carried me from the sea more dead than alive and, at the risk of his safety, brought me to this town. I ask that Mme la marquise intercede for that good Christian's life for which, in recompense, I shall place mine for ever at her service, so God help me."

She put out her gloved hand to the officer and turned.

"Why do you ask this of her?"

"Because her kindness is notorious."

The officer raised an eyebrow. The ladies-in-waiting fluttered.

She was now some nineteen or twenty years of age. I saw in fright the marks of sorrow in her face. I had carried a portrait of a young girl for ever turning her head to smile at me down the gallery of the Royal Bank at Paris. She had passed through her prisons and shipwrecks.

I went down on one knee.

She said: "Have you asked this grace of His Grandeur?"

"Not with success."

"Sir, you have your answer."

"Indeed, madame." Her equerry had had enough. "Alas! The runaway slave named François Delacour is this very moment at the port ..."

I was running. My head spun with the scent of the ladies' jasminwater and the smell of the horses. I felt such fear and horror and, surging up in the midst of it, a sensation of good fortune that I thought my heart must stop. In my fancy, I saw a cabin in the woods, shook the sweat from my eyes, bent over the haft of my pick-axe, to watch Jaan Begum under a banana palm, in a shift of blue calico and a flame-coloured turban, her baby at her sunburnt breast. As I reached the dock, my cabin in the air disintegrated.

There was a 24-pound cannon on the dock, with a broken carriage, and strapped to the gun the remains of a naked black man. His back was a ruin of clagged blood and flies. His nose and teeth had broken against the metal. At the end of the dock, a half-dozen common soldiers were sharing a bottle.

"For your bottle, friends, I will give you a piastre."

I reached in my breast for Father Patrick's purse, but where I thought there were coins was just a great musket ball or wall-gun shot wrapped in calf-leather.

My world tumbled down. One of the soldiers stood up, and handed me the bottle.

"God bless you, soldier."

I turned the bloody head and poured the liquor into the mouth. It bubbled up and spilled in streaks down the chin. I saw that François' neck was broken. I tried to close his eyes but they would not shut. I lay down beside the cannon and fell asleep.

XVIII

I woke in a somersault.

"Did you kick me, sir?"

"It was more of an ill-natured stumble. I do not much care for rising before dawn, even for the prettiest lady on earth. I am to convey you to Mme la marquise."

"I am covered in blood."

"The universal property of islands, I have heard, is that they are surrounded by water."

He had the footman's gift of lounging bolt upright.

My lady's apartments were on the left- or sea-face of the Government House, which was new-built of a wood black as jet. The room was open to the air on three sides, or rather onto a board terrace where, in a bath hollowed from a tree, parti-coloured songbirds were plashing and bickering. Every now and then during my interview, Mme de Maurepas would shoot a glance at the birds as if she heard a new or alien voice.

Mme de Maurepas was seated at a writing-desk. She had on besicles of horn, tied at the back of her hair with a ribbon, which she did not remove. It was as if she wished to be as plain as a pikestaff, though her dress was of Masulipatnam chintz with a pattern of flowers which fell to her slippered feet. Her ladies sat on tabourets, while an Indian secretary stood behind her with a wee scritor hung on a cord about his neck. The other furniture was, in the near corner, a keyboard instrument with its legs in bowls of water.

"Do you have gloves of white satinette, Mr Neilson?"

"I have no property, my lady."

"You are to clothe and equip the Chevalier Neilson as befits his birth and character."

I heard scratching from the secretary.

"What is your nation, Mr Neilson?"

"I am Scottish, my lady."

"The gentleman is Scottish? Is it difficult to be Scottish, sir? Or might one, by long study and experiment, achieve a passable Scottishness?"

"M. le chevalier Durfort, I am attempting to establish matters of fact and do not wish to hear your sour and carping tongue."

Mr Durfort appeared used to being scolded. As for the marquise, how could a girl of nineteen speak as she did? She doubted not her rank, and had learned habits of command at her father's knee, but where he was a bully, she listened and acted. Whatever you know, I know more. Whatever you have suffered, I have suffered more.

"Madame?" The younger of the ladies-in-waiting put an imaginary violin to her chin.

"Of course, like all Scottish men, he knows music."

"Yes, madame."

The ladies clapped their hands.

"The bag-pipe of Scotland!"

For a second time, I saw Mme de Maurepas smile.

"Yes, but I do not believe there is such an instrument in the île de France. I can scrape a violin, if there is one such on the island, and Mme la marquise so commands."

Her shoulders trembled. It was as if she were exhausted. She said: "Does he have any requests of her?"

"Two. That poor François be buried in consecrated ground."

"She cannot grant that. And?"

"Two silver pieces of eight."

"We shall be ruined!"

"M. le chevalier! Desist! Two?"

"Two."

"Granted. M. Neilson is to have two piastres."

The secretary scratched.

"Now," and here Mme de Maurepas took on an air of brightness, "since we must not neglect our education in this place, I shall speak to the Chevalier Neilson in his mother tongue, if I can remember any words of it."

The ladies grumbled, as if Mme de Maurepas had sworn dreadful oaths.

She turned and said in English: "A countryman of yours has wrot from Venice."

"Mr Law!"

She nodded.

"He is alive?"

"I do not know." Mme de Maurepas took from her desk a letter, which did not appear fresh. She put a hand to her spectacles and read: "I attend the opera each night, and find a pleasure to be quite alone, without servant or equipage, and to go everywhere on foot without being noted any more than any other particular citizen. In truth, madame, I prefer a sequester'd life with a small competency to all the employments and honours that the King of France could heap upon me."

She stopped, turned the sheet, and added, in an altered tone: "The grace I ask of you, madame, is this: should young Mr Neilson come to the île de France, which is my hope, he is to sail with the first vessel of the Company to Bengale. Here-attached is my bill for 500 gold louis on Mr Jogot Chet, Gentile merchant at Calcutta, with which he is to buy stock for Manila. There he shall await the arrival of the galleon from Mexico, where he will buy silver piastres and take them to Canton and exchange them for gold in ingots. He will then bring the gold to Bengale. His profit will be between fifty and eighty *per centum*. With that, he will be able to take a share in a voyage within the Indies."

She passed me the bill. On the back were eight or nine endorsements of diminishing credit or none at all, except the last: J. Maurepas in black ink that sparkled.

"But we are boring the Chevalier Durfort."

The Chevalier smiled. "Mme de Maurepas, he was born bored."

The older lady-in-waiting, Mme de Bussy, was a relation of Mme de Maurepas. She was either unmarried or widowed. The younger, Mme de Patelin, was the wife of the adjoint governor, M. le comte de Patelin. M. le chevalier Durfort, captain of engineers, had been charged with erecting a fort at the entrance to the harbour, but had in some fashion deserted the Governor and enlisted with his lady. Their usual place of residence was the île Bourbon, some forty leagues to the west-south-west which was, it appears, a Paris compared to this place. They had come in a day with the spring mousson and must wait for the autumn to go back, or labour a month or more at sea.

At noon, Mme de Maurepas rose to attend her husband. As she left the room, I said to the Chevalier:

"Sir, at some date, rather sooner than later, you and I shall have a meeting."

Mme de Maurepas spun round. She said: "If there is any quarrelling, gentlemen, let alone resort to weapons, I vow before God that you shall both be sent in irons back to the metropolis. M. Maurepas is here the representative of His Majesty and I would have you remember that. Do you understand, Mr Neilson?"

"Yes, my lady."

I was lodged, alike the Chevalier, in the guard-house. I had a bed to myself beneath a gaze curtain, and fell at once into sleep. I woke at sundown to find on the window-ledge an unsealed letter. It had in it two silver piastres and a note, which read: "Reverend father, Were you to accede to Mr Neilson's Christian request, you would oblige J. Maurepas." I supped with the men and made my way down to the dock. François was where I had left him, and my friends were seated about a fire.

"Here is the piece of money that last night I promised. There is another for you, if you will do me a further service."

The minister's house was a single room hard by the little kirk. The door opened on a friar of, I think, the Lazarite order. He was eating his supper for there were crums of bread on his black cassak. I handed him the letter. He held up his lantern to read it, then looked at me and, over my shoulder, at the littar-bearers.

I said: "If, reverend father, you should have a mind to take a turn about, or retire to your bed, none shall hear of it."

"M. Neilson, I am the parish priest. Go with your friends and prepare the ground. I shall attend you."

It was hard enough work in the moonshine, breaking the sod with bayonets. After a while, men joined us, pushing us gently aside and digging the soil with their hands. They were black men in torn clothes. We stepped back to admit Father Borthon, speaking a Latin psalm that began *De profundis*. Looking up, outside the fence, I saw trees populous with African women, girls and infants.

Dawn was breaking when I reached the guard-house. Before it was a carriage. Mme de Bussy put her head through the window.

"M. Neilson! At your garden so early!"

"I have indeed been digging, madame."

She passed through a bundle. It was a suit of linen and top-clothes.

"Dear madame, I did not expect such kindness. I have no right to it."

Mme de Bussy smiled. "Sometimes, Mr Neilson, it is hard to descry what is pleasing to God. But to clothe a naked, ship-wrecked boy, who is also my lady's pet, well, even I can see that to be religious."

Her eyes were misty. She regained command of herself. "If you will permit me, I shall be your instructress in the manners of Courts. Would you like that?"

"Very much, madame."

"I have found just two aspects of your deportment that would bear correcting. When my lady speaks to you, you are to look directly at her with a frank and open countenance. You are not to turn away your eyes."

"I understand. I am not used to the society of ladies."

"The second is that you should try to speak a little more softly. Ladies do not like to be shouted at."

"I shall try, madame."

"Otherwise, just be yourself. Who could possibly wish for any change in you?"

XIX

Mr Law had designed to use the île de France, which the Hollanders had called Mauritius after the prince or Stadholder who had led their fight for independency, because the anchorage at Bourbon was unsafe, and there was on that steep isle little land suitable for growing provisions. At Port-Louis, or the Camp, as it was called, situated at twenty degrees, ten minutes south and fifty-five degrees east, meridian of Paris, it was possible to enter and leave on a quartering wind.

At the time of my arrival on the island, in the year 1727, the town of Port-Louis was home to some nine hundred Europeans and Indians and about twice that number of Africans. A single thorofare ran up from the harbour, scattered with crazy wooden houses. The Chevalier Durfort had laid out streets on either side with cords, as we say. Lowering over it was a red mountain that they called the Thumb.

The cits were idle and frightened to death of the slaves. They talked incessantly of returning to the metropolis, and whiled away their hours in small speculations in an open space called the place d'Armes. Chief among the speculators was the Governor himself, and his pal favourite, the comte de Patelin. There was little coin, and if Spanish piastres appeared in trade, or pagodas from Pondicherry, they vanished into hoards. The principal currencies were the notes of the King, signed by Mr Maurepas for the expenses of the military establishment. They were known as Roys and traded at discounts to face of as much as sixty *per centum*. The bills of hand of his lady, which were called, by the same system, Madames, traded at a five *per centum* agio or premium over cash. I was told they were good for silver at Malacca and at Canton.

Between the two species of paper, there was a to-and-fro or arbitrage. It was thought that my ship, the *Prince-de-Conty*, had called at Cadix to buy silver piastres for the garrison and, as soon as our sail appeared to the south, the Place sold the Madames and bought the Roys. At the wreck, the trade went into reverse and there were many men with burns on their thumbs. Mme de Maurepas displayed no knowledge of this undignified commerce.

She it was who had brought from Paris the two coaches and from Muscate their teams. She had built the Government House, employing the ship's carpenters of the dismasted *Mutine*, in part to seat the Provincial Council, as ripe a collection of blackguards as may be found this side of Aberdeen. To please her, skippers brought her bricks in ballast, Indian cattle, grains such as dry rice and maize, and medicinal or nourishing plants that might flourish on the island. Behind the Government House, Mme de Maurepas had established a pepinier or tree nursery to nurture those plants. She disliked the wretched fences of wood in the camp, which the cattle broke with their heads. Under her direction, the Chevalier and I planted a hedge of roses brought from Macau by the captain of the *Amphitrite*. I wondered if, by her marriage settlement, Mme de Maurepas had not retained the free disposition of her fortune.

To escape the heat, we rose with the light. By the time the Chevalier and I rattled into the drawing-room at six of the morning, Mme la marquise was at her desk, writing letters that might not be sent for months. She heard our reports, allocated our tasks and, at the slightest sign of gaiety, so natural to young persons, reminded us of our duty. At mid-morning, the Chevalier left to superintend the work on his fort. It was an Arras in reduction, so to speak, and of black timber and red earth rather than brick and stone. M. le marquis de Vauban would have applauded. Mme de Maurepas wished it soon completed so as to pass on to her preferred scheme of a dispensary.

After dinner, the ladies drove out. There the famous white gloves came into service. As the ladies mounted the carriage, we were to take the pleats of their dresses without marking them with unwholesome masculine sweat. We then bumped and stumbled about the little town, the ladies in the open carriage, the Chevalier and I riding straight as spokes, looking neither to left nor to right. Since there were few visits to pay or repay, we generally found ourselves at sundown in a prairie on the edge of town, where the Chevalier and I fanned the grasses for insects to take to Mme la marquise for what she called classification. The purpose was to set an example of industry to an hang-arse population. It was make-believe sustained not by nature, reason or prospect of gain but by the will of one young married woman. It was as if an angel had stopped at a murderers' inn.

When I was dull or moped, Mme de Maurepas would say: "Courage, Mr Neilson! The Company ships will come with the mousson and you shall soon be among your silks and chintzes."

I submitted my report on the wreckage of the *Prince-de-Conty* to the Provincial Council. Mme de Maurepas was kind enough to give me leave to visit the place of wreckage. Fearing that I would not find the place by land, I took on her order the government chaloupe or long-boat and six Africans to man the oars. It was a whole day's coasting, the men in dreadful fear but sticking to their task and singing brave songs. At the île d'Ambre, I gave them cloths soaked in vinegar, and we buried above the tide what remains we could find. I encouraged the men to take for themselves any nails, coins or other metal jetsome brought by the waves. That night we made a bivouac on the beach and sang songs of our several nations. On the morrow, as I was launching the boat into the suffe, I saw, spinning in the foam, a bottle of Champagne. I opened it, poured a libation to the soul of my martyred friend, then gave the men to drink in their cupped hands.

XX

One morning, a good month after my arrival at Port-Louis, we came to the drawing-room to find, perched on a stand like a shiny parrot, a violin.

"See, Mr Neilson, I have found your fiddle."

"I am ravished to see so fine an instrument on the island."

"I did not know it had been brought from Bourbon. It is by Stainer of Innsbruck. It was my mother's. I know you will have a care of it. The ants here are connoisseors of stringed instruments."

"May I tune it, my lady?"

It was as if I had mounted a thoroughbred horse.

Exhilarated by its touch, I played the first bars of a strathspey that the Highland men used to strike at end of day when they stopped with their beasts at Grandfather's farm. I looked up. The Chevalier was bolt upright, the ladies on their toes. Mme la marquise was half-way from her chair.

"O Mr Neilson, will you not show me how to play it?"

At her spinet, she picked up the down-beat at once. As I turned, I saw the ladies extemporising steps. Mme de Maurepas stood up and closed the cover of the spinet.

"Ladies and gentlemen! What are we, rioting in plain morning!"

"Madame?"

There was something, in the air or space between the marquise and the countess. We others might not have existed.

"There is no room of sufficient size either for the dancers or for supper. What shall the ladies wear? Where shall we find other musicians? Mme de Patelin, you have not considered your project in all its aspects." And then, with grace: "Granted."

The countess whooped.

Mme de Maurepas said: "Ladies and gentlemen, for His Majesty's birthday there shall be a dancing-party at Port-Louis, the first I believe among Europeans though not, I am sure, the indigenous or the blacks."

As she stood up to leave, I said:

"While you dine, my lady, do you wish me to tune the spinetta?"

"No. I do not play."

The dancing-party was all our occupation. The Chevalier proposed to use the torn sails and broken spars in the marine store to make two pavilions, the one for dancing, the other for supper, and made some drawings for Mme la marquise to approve. I was to riffle the town for musical instruments and musicians. We were excused attendance on the levy, which had become unbearably furtive and feminine. Our carriage rides prolonged to sundown, for there was every house to be visited. Fine Indian cloth there was, and cutters and seamsters enough, but no patterns. Mme de Bussy, who was held to be adept in the secrets of the rue des Bourdonnais at Paris, was much in requirement.

I found three violins and a 'cello among the European families, but none to play them. In the African town, I was better successful.

"My lady, your musicians are waiting on the terrace for your orders."

The men stood in the sunlight, barefoot, heads bowed, hats in their hands.

"What are you doing, Mr Neilson?"

"I am doing my best, my lady."

Mme de Maurepas spoke up: "You do not have to play at the dancing-party. If you wish to do so, and your masters consent, you shall receive from me each man a suit of clothes, a hat and a pair of shoes."

There was a mumble of thank-yees.

XXI

There being no coaches apart from those of Mme la gouvernante, the ladies arrived in palanquins or littars, each carried by four African men, with another four shuffling behind as relays. For an hour or so, the tente was a patter of praise and compliments, for the ladies of the île de France are gay and good-natured. The governor sat with his gossibs at the head. As the evening advanced, the heat, the tallow-smoak, the squadrones of children, and the arrack-punch began to take a toll on the elegance of the affair. Faces shone like beacon-fires. Toilettes dragged or fluttered while some of the gentlemen snored in their elbow-chairs like stags in the rut.

For the first time, I was able to inspect M. and Mme de Maurepas together. Accustomed to that lady's absolute government, I was not prepared for her homage to M. Maurepas. Everything she did or said seemed designed to enforce his authority or to augment his comfort. If a chair were unsteady or a bottle spoiled or a pal failed to smile at his pleasanterie, Mme de Maurepas set it to rights. I sought, with a lover's eagerness, a hint of self-performance, but could not find it.

"No, no, M. Patelin. Trajan was a Roman emperor. There is no such ancient city as Tray."

As for M. Maurepas, he might have been a child and my lady his mam.

My orchestra was not as I had hoped. The second violin had been struck by his overseer and the thumb of his left hand broke. He had sent as his substitute a lively, handsome young man of about twenty years of age. We had no sheet music, and anyway none could read it, but the neophyte followed me to the note.

"Mr Neilson! The Scottish contre danse, if you please!"

"At your service, Mme de Patelin. Will you not show the company the steps?"

The countess and the Chevalier stepped out. They must have rehearsed for days. They danced as I had never seen dancing and withal so chaste that it took the breath away.

"Will you not lead the dance, Mr Governor?"

M. de Maurepas scowled and looked ahead of him.

I saw that he detested not only me but all his lady's little philosophical Court. I wondered if it had to do with money. Mme de Maurepas stood up.

She said: "I shall dance as your depute. Mr Neilson and Mr Stainer of Innsbruck will lead me."

Mme de Maurepas danced with only the slightest movement, but perfectly in step with the music. She seemed to see nothing. It was as if her eyes were fixed on a point in the ocean. My hands being occupied with my fiddle, I could not touch her. I suppose that was her intention.

In my reverie, I felt that something was not right. I looked at the orchestra, and saw that the alternate violinist was standing. Though he had easily mastered the beat, he had a mind to improve it, and sallied off in every tempo and key, before returning like a sight-hound of which one had despaired. The dancing began to disintegrate. With a frank and open expression, I looked into my dancing-partner's face. I did not speak.

Mme de Maurepas, may I say something to you?

You may say nothing to me that others cannot hear.

Mme de Maurepas stopped dead. "What is that man doing?"

She turned and glared at the delinquant fiddler. He bowed his head. The dancers halted in mid-step. I picked up the dance, and all went well enough, except the violinist now played with a timid and pettifogging accuracy, like a spoiled pupil or a serinette.

Mme de Maurepas stopped and walked back to the seated guests. Over her shoulder, she said: "No doubt, Mr Neilson, my dinted feet and ankles will repair. See that the musicians are given refreshment." As the orchestra stood to bow to her, she discharged a look of flame.

I took the players into a back-part. The Indian servants refused to wait on them so I brought their meat and drink myself. At first, they would touch nothing, but then the bold violinist took a sip of wine, and soon there was the munching and quaffing of men who do not know when they shall break their fast again.

The violinist raised his glass to me.

I said: "What is your name, Mr Fiddler?"

"My Christian name is Ézéchiel."

"You are twice the musician I am, M. Ézéchiel."

"Shall you come to our town one Sunday eve to play at our dances?"

"With the greatest pleasure. I shall ask Jaan Begum's permission."

Which was refused. At Waiting the next morning, Mme de Maurepas turned in her chair and said:

"Attention, ladies and gentleman, for I am to reprimand Mr Neilson."

"Ah madame, should you not do that in private interview?" That was kind Mme de Bussy.

"I do not care to be in private with Mr Neilson, or with any man except my lord. Now, sir, why do you think I consented to have dancing?"

"I do not know, my lady."

"Do you think I like dancing?"

"Not at all, my lady."

"I staged the entertainment not to please myself or you, but so that word might pass into the metropolis that there is a very little society at Port-Louis. I hoped by that scheme and others to overcome, among persons of condition in France, a reluctance to come here, and thus, in a feminine way, to support my lord and His Majesty. Now, Mr Neilson, do you think that your project of playing Malagasy airs in the slave-town will help or hinder my scheme?"

"Hinder, my lady."

"I do not care for your religious or philosophical scruples. His Majesty has permitted African slavery in the isles and that is all you need to know."

Mme de Maurepas glared at me through her eyeglasses. She said: "You do not have to remain in my service, Mr Neilson. You may leave with honour, and live among the blacks and play their music to your heart's content.

If you wish to stay, you must obey my every instruction; and, Mr Neilson, I would have you think a little more and act a little less."

"As you command, my lady."

"Come now, M. Neilson, do not be downcast. I have also praise for you. You were the first to recognise that man's genius. In speaking to his master, M. Dugros, I learn that M. Ézéchiel is a better musician than he is field-worker. M. Dugros is not especially musical, and I have bought from my pin-money his slave's freedom. My intention was to send M. Ézéchiel, again at my expense, to be formed at Paris. I could not win M. Maurepas to that plan but I have succeeded to the extent that henceforth our little orchestra will consist only of free-born or liberated men. M. Neilson will direct until such time as he leaves for India, and will prepare M. Ézéchiel to succeed him in that dignity."

"Thank you, my lady."

"Are we now friends?"

"We were never not friends, my lady."

"Ladies and gentlemen! Original Genius is born in a shed as well as in a palace, and to black as to white skin. It will always make itself known. Our task is to promote not Genius but those of more common or everyday ability, such as Mr Neilson."

"You are kind, my lady."

XXII

"His Grandeur is required at Bourbon. With his permission, I am to remain here to pursue the works I have set on foot."

Her ladies-in-waiting blenched. "What about the guard?"

"His Grandeur's life guard attends him."

The Chevalier said: "I never really cared for Bourbon. I rather think I shall stay and build my fort."

"And I, my lady. Mr Law believed that the île de France was by much the better suited to serve as the Company's victualling station."

"You are well-instructed about your countryman's intentions, Mr Neilson. You said you had been his under-clerk."

Mme la marquise de Maurepas, during the single evening I served Mr Law, I took the dictation of four letters. Two were procurations or powers-of-attorney over lands, manors and fabricks in Normandie. The third, which was addressed to M. le comte de Toulouse, secretary of the Marine, debated the several merits of île Bourbon and île de France as port of call for the ships of the Company and the King. The fourth I have forgot.

I stepped back into rank. I said: "Mr Law's reasoning

on the question was common knowledge even among his lower servants."

Mme de Maurepas shook off her humour.

"Heavens, gentlemen! What have I done to deserve such fidelity?"

"And we shall stay to amuse you."

"But Mme la comtesse! Your husband goes to Bourbon!"

Once again, there was that secret between them.

"I believe my duty is to serve you."

There was silence. Mme la marquise de Maurepas was lost in thought.

"Shall you enforce the Code, madame?"

Mme de Maurepas started from her dream. "Yes, but without affectation. Do you know what that means, Mr Neilson: without affectation?"

"I think it means, my lady, that I am to go to the African town and say to one or other, as by way of pleasanterie: Such are the punishments permitted by the King, and such the minimum daily nourishment set by his decrees. If the first be exceeded, and the second fall short, they should at once be reported to Mme la gouvernante . . ."

". . . for immediate conveyance to His Grandeur and the Provincial Council."

"I understand."

"Can you do that for me, Mr Neilson? I know it is not the Scottish way, but it is the French."

"Yes, my lady."

"I have heard that many ladies find a side-arm becoming."

"Oh come, M. le chevalier. We shall shoot off our toes. Are we not friends of their darling Mr Neilson, and as safe as in the rue du Bac?"

"As you command, madame."

XXIII

Once Mr Maurepas and his general staff had departed, a sort of flatness of temper fell on the place. I had expected that we would be much engaged, but that was not the case, which caused me to think that the Governor's officers had not been especially active. I sensed that Mme la marquise de Maurepas had no wish to innovate, but rather to give more manage, as we say. The star-fort sprang forward, like a greyhound off the leash. Whatever was holding up the engineering, it had sailed away.

As the member of Mme la gouvernante's general staff with the greatest commercial expertise (which, as the reader will recollect, amounted to a whole evening with Mr Law of Lauriston at the Royal Bank at Paris), I was given controle of the finances. I made an inspection of the stores, interrogated the keepers and called up the ledgers, such as they were. I was as taciturn as Rhadamanthus. I refused all gestures of hospitality.

At Waiting, I said: "My lady, may I request the favour of a private audience so as to present the finances?"

"That shall not be necessary, Mr Neilson. Draw up a memorial and, as far as you are able, strike a balance."

The finances do not balance, my lady.

Strike the balance none the less, Mr Neilson.

I did as I was told. The next day, Mme de Maurepas returned me my memorial with her bill on Paris to cover the lacunae. Active and passive now balanced.

The ladies, weary of the dispensary, dreamed of a social occasion so as to display, to white and black, a hardie nonchalance and to protract or prolong the spirit of the dancing-party. They dreamed of horse-races without horses, tennis without a ball and regatte without boats.

"Do you have a proposal, Mr Neilson?"

"Yes, my lady."

"Make your proposal, Mr Neilson, if you please."

"In my country, on the borderlands of Scotland and England, it is the practice one day in the fair season ..."

"There is a fair season in Scotland?"

". . . to make a sort of assembly on the river bank, or on the greens, to which none is invited and all are welcome so long as each brings some provision, such as snuff, or ale, or strong waters, or a violin. One of the better farmers might contribute a hogg, or an angleman a pair fine salmon. There in the open air, there are foot-races and archery . . .

"Hurry! Let us leaf through our Theocritus!"

". . . and bowling and cache and such alike innocuous games. It is on such days that the young men and maidens come to their understandings . . ."

"Heaven forbid that the race of Caledonia should die out!"

". . . the old fellows prose and souse, the dames critick, the lasses twirl, while the younger lads repair to the woods, there to enact scenes of North American valour and cruelty."

"What do you call such a rural fête, Mr Neilson?"

"We call it a kettle."

"And have you a place in mind for your chaudron, Mr Neilson?"

"Yes, my lady. When I came first to Port-Louis, passing under the Thumb, I crossed a wide lawn that had been browsed by cattle. From it, there is a fair view over the town with the harbour and the open sea in the distance, and a sea-wind to abate the sun's heat."

"Thank you, Mr Neilson. I believe such a rural jaunt might reinforce that sense of union so evident at the dancing-party."

"Shall you attend, madame?"

"The affair, I am afraid, is beneath His Grandeur's dignity. You shall represent him and shall do very well."

The Chevalier spoke up. "My lady, when I was last at that place, I was struck by the colour and variety of nature's palette. There were lawns and woods and prairie, and spiny thicket and also rocky slopes in which all manner of repellent, crawling creatures were sunning themselves at His Christian Majesty's expense."

"M. le chevalier, I did not know you cared for natural history." She paused. "Very well, I shall attend the fête, but in a spirit of science rather than pleasure."

"Madame, is this not an occasion to entertain His Majesty's Mohammedan and Gentile subjects?"

"Well said, Mme de Bussy. This excursion will have none of the exclusive character of the dancing-party."

"The dance was exclusive?"

"M. le chevalier! We are not, at present, at Sceaux."

"I have, for a time, begun to suspect that."

XXIV

On the morrow, at dawn, Mr Durfort and I rode out to inspect the road up to the Thumb. Once we were out of the houses, I said:

"Shall we not today have our meeting?"

"I am not aware, M. Neilson, of any quarrel between us."

"I observed you smiling during my reprimand."

"I smiled at Mme la marquise's character of M. Dugros: that of all that gentleman's faults of person, formation and moral sentiments, she selected for notice only his lack of musical education. Besides, were we to meet, you would be killed and I would be banished the society of Mme la marquise de Maurepas."

"Are you calling me a poor swordsman, sir?"

"Not at all. I am saying that my seniority and military education will outweigh your undoubted valour."

"Admit you do not like me."

"On the contrary, I find you an addition to our little society. Your conduct in the matter of the runaway displayed a rude, septentrional merit. I find, even, that Mme la marquise is on occasion harsh with you."

"Do you dare to upbraid our mistress, sir?"

"By no means. It is just that the lady's desire to reinforce her husband and keep good order in society leads her to a sternness painful to those who love her."

"Ah! Admit that you love her."

"I should take care, M. Neilson. Those are dangerous waters."

". . . and you design to dishonour her for your own reckless pride and pleasure."

"M. Neilson, that is a disgusting insult. By God, you shall withdraw that."

"I shall not."

The Chevalier made an effort of self-command. "We may not fight, M. Neilson, because you do not have a witness to act for you."

"One of the blacks will stand for me." I had in mind Mr Ézéchiel.

M. le chevalier Durfort sighed. "Alright, M. Neilson, I shall fight you, if that is what you want, and kill you, if you want that also, but not while we are under the law and dominion of Mme de Maurepas."

"I might waylay you in a cowardly fashion and oblige you to defend yourself. Then, if you kill me, you shall not be reprimanded."

"There, M. Neilson, I believe you are spinning the thread of honour too fine. We shall not fight here, sir. I have given the lady my word, and so have you. Let us talk of other matters. Above all, how we are to bring carts up this foolish mountain, including those of M. Mousa Solimane and his extensive, even limitless, household. I would wish you to consider that, should you assassinate me, you will have to do a double duty."

I hated Mr Durfort, not just for my lady's favour, but for his insouciance. Yet you cannot work a whole day in burning sun with a man without some understanding of his nature. Beneath the fop was an engineer of merit. He showed me how to cut and bind fascines to enforce the road where the innumerable rills and burns had broken it, and hold them in place with stakes he called in his military technology *chandeliers*. He spoke no more, except at noon, where he straightened and said: "I am rather coming round to the notion of African slavery."

XXV

The fête had nothing Tweedside about it, but was not without its charm. The Chevalier and I set up camp a day in advance, so as to erect awnings for Mme la gouvernante, a place for the band of my musicians to play, and a screened enclosure for the Mussulmane ladies and their infants.

The kettle itself was thought a littell Scotch and rustic, and so we dug pits to roast a whole beef and broil bonites. From our vantage, we watched the cavalcade, led by the Government coach, winding its way up from the town.

At first, there was a sort of coasting tendency, in which each family kept close to the safety of its near acquaintance, but Mme de Maurepas and her ladies moved between each knot of people and sought by word or gesture to combine them. I could see over my musicians' heads the bobbling of her ombrelle. Children ran up to her, always with the same tree-fearn, which she examined with minute interest. The sun blazed, the smoke from the pits blew, the music gusted, and there was much resort to the arrack-punch.

Mme de Patelin oversaw the dancing and pans'd the injur'd feet. I saw the gentleman who had shot at me and ponder'd a scheme to make him ridiculous. A little later, I watched Mme de Maurepas and Mme de Bussy walking towards the enclosure of the Mussulmane ladies. They returned, after half an hour, in the highest spirits. The Chevalier Durfort waylaid them. He pointed to the sky where, from the direction of the town, a black cloud was sidling towards us.

I said: "My lady, before we decamp, Mr Ézéchiel begs to be permitted to sing for you."

Mme de Maurepas nodded her head, but remained standing.

Mr Ézéchiel unwrapped an instrument, somewhat alike to the cithara of the ancient Greeks, but strung on what appeared to be a great bambou. Using a plectrum, he struck a chord, and then, as his auditors waited, closed his eyes. The song when it came was of the softest so that every person fell silent, holding breath, straining to hear. The Mussulmane ladies and children crowded the door of their enclosure. Once again, Mr Ézéchiel ranged from key to key, like a workman moving between his benches, but always returned to the point at which he had started. The song ended as softly as it had begun, leaving an echo of something remote or far gone in the past. Mr Ézéchiel opened his eyes, shivered and turned to me.

I said: "The words mean, my lady: Ézéchiel was a slave, and suffered the whip and chain and collar and iron boot. But now, now that he is a freed man, alas, his condition is worse, for he is enslaved to . . ."

"I know what the words mean, Mr Neilson." She turned to the singer. "M. Ézéchiel, you are quite as good a singer as you are a player. We are fortunate to have you. Now, let us make haste before the rain. Ladies! Kindly ensure that you have all your children with you."

Without turning, Mme de Maurepas said: "What are you doing, Mr Neilson?"

"I am trying to know your will."

"Ladies! Please be quite certain that your children are with you. M. Neilson, and M. Durfort, will you beat the brakes and bushes and flush out any laggards?"

As I was scouring the horizon, something crept over my left boot. I placed the right boot atop it.

"My lady," I croaked. "I have the viper."

Mme de Maurepas turned, looked at me, and at my one-legged stance, and began to run towards me. Her ladies came bustling after. They found me swaying like a scatter-craw in a gale. The ladies-in-waiting shrieked.

"Mme de Bussy, would you have the kindness to bring me a clean and dry wine-glass?"

"No!" Mesdames de Bussy and de Patelin were running away.

"Females!"

Mme de Maurepas belonged, it seems, of a sex of one, with the privileges of the other two, but none of their faults.

"M. le chevalier! Kindly bring me the glass and send the people away. Mme de Bussy will conduct them."

Mme de Maurepas put on her spectacles.

I said: "May I speak, my lady?"

"Do not speak, Mr Neilson. Or you will kill me."

"I must speak!"

"No. Reach down and take the tail of the creature and hold it at arm's length."

The Chevalier Durfort returned with the wine-glass. "Could you not let the worm sting me, and then extract the poison from my corpse?"

"The venom would be contaminated, and I will have lost a dear friend. Do hold the creature still, Mr Neilson, and shake a little less. I am relieved that you are destined for the civilian and not the military profession."

I all but threw the reptile at her.

Wrapping her Cachemire about her hand, Mme de Maurepas advanced the glass in a cirkling motion. The snake swayed in imitation, this side and that, then locked its jaws on the rim. A dark liquid oozed and siped down the glass.

"Mr Neilson, it is especially your friends the blacks who suffer from this creature. If I can make an analyse, thereby separating the venom into its constituent elements, then I shall have a firmer idea of how to treat their snake-stings."

The liquid had ceased to flow. "Now," Mme de Maurepas said, "we must leave the creature with a portion of its venom or it shall starve."

I cast the wicked thing into the brakes.

Turning, I saw the Chevalier handing Mme de Maurepas into the coach. He tied his horse to the back-rail, and took the coachman's seat. I mounted and sculked along behind.

It began to rain, and soon the hillside was bubbling with water the colour of iron rust. To compound my misery, I was soaking wet. As the coach jolted round a corner, the off-side wheel sagged, the fascine slid and broke and the coach crumpled on its broken axle. The door sprang open, spilling bottles and jars. I spurred into air. Mme la marquise collided with my saddle and I caught her by the waist. Her touch made me swoon while, to her, my arms might have been molten lead. My mount was losing his footing. Across the gill, Mr Durfort was descending in giant's bounds.

"Cast Her Ladyship to me, William!"

I had been aware of Mr Newton's Third Law, but only by theory. I now experienced it in praxis. As Mme de Maurepas flew from my arms, my horse slid back and fell on its rump. As I rolled clear, I caught the flying reins, which snapped in my hand. We tumbled down the burn through a litter of spiny leaves. Beneath was a great ebeny tree, with many stems like an outgrown coppice. With a dreadful sound, my mount landed against it on his back. A hoof hit me in the head. Gasping, we lay in the thorns.

I rose, raised the beast, knotted the reins and we set off across the slope, taking each step on its own. After a while, the timber became more sparse, and the slope less steep, and we began to climb. An hour had elapsed, or perhaps less, before we won through to our road. The rain had passed and the sun was turning all to vapour. We crept up through mists towards the carriage.

Mme la marquise de Maurepas was white as paper. At some distance, the Chevalier stood upright. They appeared to have had words.

She said: "I suppose in Scotland, Mr Neilson, a gentleman cares first for his horse and only then for his mistress."

The Chevalier Durfort made to speak and then thought better of it.

I said: "Mme de Maurepas, I can bear your unkindness no longer. Your rank, beauty and learning bestow on you certain privileges, but no right to bully a servant who cares only for your happiness."

She bit her lip. She seemed, for a moment, a mere girl far from home. In the silence, I ploughed on.

"I propose, madame, that you mount the Chevalier's horse . . ."

"I shall not sit astride a horse."

"It is the work of a moment to adjust the stirrup-irons so you can ride side-on. Mr Durfort will lead you and I shall follow, with the coach-horses and my poor mount."

"I shall not ride, Mr Neilson. You are to go down to Port-Louis and order the second coach to be brought up. The Chevalier Durfort will attend me here."

"The Chevalier's horse is sound!"

"Do you intend to disobey my order, Mr Neilson?"

"No, my lady."

I bowed to Mme Maurepas and her friend and then, with three jaded horses and a broken heart, I plodded away downhill.

"Mr Neilson!"

I stopped and did a half-turn.

"Forgive me."

"There is nothing to forgive, Mme de Maurepas."

"There is."

As I came to the slope above the town, I saw marching up the road towards me a troop of marines. Beyond, a ship was anchored in the rode.

"Good work, gentlemen. The coach is overthrown and Mme la gouvernante is shaken but not injured. I am to bring the reserve coach."

The officer pushed aside his gaberdine and raised his piece at my chest.

I plunged among the horses and found my pistol-holster. It was empty.

(She has disarmed me.)

I felt a pain in my skull such as I had never known.

(She has killed me.)

PART 4

Pondichéry or Pondicherry, 1727

XXVI

I became conscious of darkness, of pain and of wetness. I thought the wetness might be my blood, but it tasted salt. I was lying in a sort of hutch of deal planks, in the gaps of which I could see light and feel air and salt water. I was on ship-board. (She has sent me away with my life.)

On the crown of my head was a bump good to show at the Fair. I thought back to my last moments of conscience, on the road about Port-Louis. I was alive, which was not nothing, but all my projects had fallen down. My love for Mme de Maurepas, and the hope that one day, at what time in the future so ever, we might be united, which had sustained me since I had first come into France, had come to nothing. I would not know that happiness that only a woman can bestow. Solitude would be my mistress.

I saw that I must take my first steps in that solitary life.

I saw that I must forgive Mme de Maurepas or that life would be unbearable. Women have the right to entertain preferences, and to seek what happiness as can be found in this world below. Married to a man who is her inferior in everything, is it a wonder that Mme la Marquise looks about her?

My heart revolted at this reasoning. In truth, I did not believe it. She had sent me away for fear that I would destroy her world. I believed she loved me and that I loved her, and we would, one day, in our passages through life, meet again. With that, heart and mind resolved upon a truce.

I took stock. I had never had much property, but now I had none, except my sodden clothes and Mr Law's bill. Then I bethought me of Father O'Crean's pock about my neck. I opened the gut-string. In it was an irregular sphere, as much the size of a gowf ball but twice or thrice as heavy. It had something of the look of clouded glass. I turned it in the palm of my hand.

My beating head returned to the Royal Bank at Paris, and the letters I had written at Mr Law's dictation. The last, which I had forgotten or, perhaps, put away for later consideration, had been addressed to His Royal Highness the Duke of Orléans and concerned something called "this affair" or "this affair of Ireland". Mr Law proposed that the object must first be polished before His Royal Highness might judge whether the Bank should buy it for His Majesty's coronation regalia.

As far as I could see we were sailing eastwards. I laughed for I had with me an unpolished diamond worth more than the îles de France and Bourbon conjoin'd, but it did not belong to me. Nor, since Mr Law's bank had failed, did it belong to King Louis the Fifteenth. It belonged to Father Patrick's master, King James Stuart at Rome in the other or westernwards direction.

To exercise my legs, I pressed with my heels against the door of the cage, which opened. I followed my feet out, and stood up. The ship ran like a race-horse, plunging forward on only her civadier. All around were small islands scarcely raised above the sea, where creatures like giant bauckie-birds glided above clusters of trees. Skate-fish the size of calves gambolled about us on beating wings. With nothing to do, the sailors crouched on deck, spinning yarn, or knitting stockings or whittling at toys. There was a scent of cannel, as from the coffee-house in the Edinburgh Lawnmarket. I made my way to the maître-pilote at the wheel.

"Will you kindly tell me the name of this vessel, sir?"

He started. "She is *Atalante*, the finest ship in the merchant fleet."

"And her captain, if I may trouble you further?"

"The famous M. Béranger."

"How shall I find him?"

Too surprised to speak, the maître took one hand off the wheel and gestured behind him.

I came into a cabin brimming with light. From the taffrail, the ensign of the Company of the Indies flapped and rattled against the panes. Captain Béranger was leaning over a chart table, smoking a clay pipe. The smoke danced in the window light.

Through billows of smoke, he said: "For a young man, M. Neilson, you are a notably bad subject." He reached for a paper, glanced at it and then at me. "Fomented sedition among the blacks to the peril of the King's peace and the prosperity of the Company of the Indies. Introduced dissension among the French ..."

"Neither charge is just, sir."

"That is what is written in the letter under cachet, M. Neilson. The letter is signed by M. le marquis de Maurepas, an imbecile, sodomite and thief, but none the less His Majesty's governor of the île Bourbon and the île de France."

"There was a dispute over the ladies."

"No ladies here, M. Neilson, and none I fear for many hundreds of miles about. Do you have another proficiency? I mean, other than ladies."

"I have orders to make my way to Chandernagore as second-clerk and writer at the Company's factory there."

"I hope for your sake, M. Neilson, that there are ladies at Chandernagore." He tore the sealed-letter into pieces. "Kneel before me."

I did so.

"Repeat: "I swear to serve the King with honour and fidelity . . ."

"I swear to serve the King with honour and fidelity. . ."

". . . to the glory of France and the success of her arms."

". . . to the glory of France and the success of her arms."

"You may stand, Mr Ensign Neilson. You shall dine at my table with an allowance of one bottle of wine a day and half one pint of eau-de-vie. You may carry stock-in-trade for your own account up to a value of 10,000 livres landed. You will never question an order. If there is a fight, which I do not particularly intend, you will fight."

"Yes, Captain."

"M. Bolande will show you your duties."

"Sir, an hour ago I was lying in a puddle in your gaol. Now, I am the most eager of your commissioned officers. May I inquire what has brought such a revolution in my fortunes?"

Captain Béranger burst out in laughter. "You live, that is all. You shall find, M. Neilson, that in the Indies you have only to live to rise to fortune and happiness. The skill, of course, is to live."

XXVII

There were times, in the weary years that followed, when I near forgot that skill. There was the dawning day at Gingie Fort, when I carried the lighted petard to the gate. The flash is still with me. When the smoke thinned, I saw through a film of blood a host of men with brustled mustaches who dropped their firelocks in a clitter-clatter. Or, in the night attack on Trivandrum, when the skiff overthraw in the surf and I lay drowning in the shallows under a heap of dead cipayes. At those moments and others, I was so close to death I could have touched her.

What saved me, if I can make so very odd an assertion, was the Persian language. It was spoken at the Mohammedan Courts of India with any pretension to politeness, and even by some of the Hindou.

I had been sent by Mr Le Noir, the governor-general of our French establishments, to the Court of the Nawab or Governor of Tanjore to encourage that wise Prince to repay a portion of his debts. While waiting to take my leave of His Highness, and whiling away my time in the arcade before the throne room, I heard a group of gentlemen in robes-of-honour conversing in a tongue I thought was Italian. On a second hearing, I thought it was French, then Latin, then English. They broke off their speech to admit me.

"May I enquire," I said in the jargon they call Hindoustanie, "what is that beautiful language you speak?"

"It is Court speech, dear sir."

"It is much alike my mother tongue."

"That is because, dear sir, your tongue is a version, much debased, if we may be permitted to say so, of Persian."

"Or might it not be that both tongues descend from a common parent, as we are all sons of Adam?"

"You are permitted your own opinion, how far-fetched soever."

"Gentlemen, would you be so kind to recommend me a teacher of the Court language?"

"We shall be your teachers."

I never saw Chandernagore. I was discharged by Mr Béranger, entered into the land service and at once placed in command of a broken lot of English deserters, most but not all of them Scottish. They cared no more than I did for the King of France. I needed to make them care for one another.

The empire of the Great Moghol, which had raised India to a pitch of opulence not hitherto achieved on earth, was in its decadency. A hardie race of Hindou warriors, known as Mahrattes, while paying lip-service to the Emperor at Delhi, had taken command of the coasts and much of the in-land. All manner of princes and nawabs, like lairdies moving a dyke while neighbour is up to town, were seeking to extend their dominions. Mr Le Noir, the governor-general, saw some profit for the Company in supplying men and artillery. I volunteered my men for every fight and scrape, and they became good soldiers and good friends and heaped up some booty. Mr Le Noir was kind enough to allow us our own badges, and what with drums and pipes, we made a show (though nothing like the din of an Indian army on the march). After the action at Gingie, His Highness the Nawab of Tanjore granted me the right always to be preceded by four kettle-drums. Out of charity to my ears, and those of my men, I made no use of that privilege. I received the title of Toupbashi, or Master of Ordnance. In '32, after four years of indiscriminate soldiering, I was gazetted captain with the provisory rank of lieutenant-colonel.

I never made any fortune. Mr Joseph Cardoso, Portugal

merchant, loaned me a house and garden hard by the Capuchins on the edge of Pondicherry town and seemed eager to give me one or all three of his daughters. My brother officers thought to have caught a flash of black eyes in my zenanah or women's apartments, but in truth I lived as deceint a life as is possible for a soldier far from home. Each morning, at dawn, before I went to my men, one of my teachers would come to walk with me in the garden. Often, we would spend an hour on a single couplet of Haufiz, while Mr Cardoso's weavers sang away at their looms in the shade of colossal mango trees. If I dreamed in Scots, I took it for an omen and stayed within doors all day, like an ancient Roman.

Mr Cardoso told me of a diamond the size of a hen's egg, dug from the ground at Visapour in the last years of the century just past. After jumping like a frog through many hands, it came to Mr Jogot Chet, Hindou merchant of Calcutta, who sold it, for forty thousand pagodas, to an English interloper named Crean. Mr Chet had since regretted the bargane, for he had learned how great a price a flawless diamond might command amid the jealous princes of Europe. Of Mr Crean, a roughling, immoral man from Mr Cardoso's report, there had been seen not hide nor hair. Of the diamond, like-wise.

On my missions to the different Courts, I saw many

fine jewels, generally worn on the arm. As far as I could judge, they were not cut to the European taste, and were more treasured for size and heft than for purity. I could not for the life of me understand why Father Patrick had brought the jewel back to the Indies. I guess'd that he had been unable to find a cutter at Venice, Amsterdam or London, or none that he might trust. The diamond, and the cause of the royal house of Stuart, would have to wait until I had congee to return to Europe. I wrote to His Majesty at Rome, by both the *Garonne* and the *Loire*, stating that I had something of very great value to place before him and asking if he might graciously inform me of his will. Answer I received none.

PART 5

Persia, 1739

XXVIII

Because of my pleasure in the Persian language, in the month of May, 1739, Mr Du Mas, Mr Le Noir's successor as governor-general, sent me to seek a treaty of friendship with Nader Shah of Iran who had invaded the Moghol's empire and was then lording it over the Emperor's capital, Delhi. For two days, I rode through the smoke of dead fires. Having tired of weighing treasure and slitting bellies, the conqueror had marched with his army into the north and thus I made my own way into Persia.

His Majesty Shah Nader's capital, if such an institute might be attributed to so restless a prince, was the city of Mashhad, where he had poured endowments on the shrine of one of their Saints. His kingdom was in uproar, and he was for ever on campaign, either against his surly subjects or the armies of the Turkish Sultan or the khans

of Transoxiania. In vain I sought an audience. Lodged
with me in a corner of the palace were an English cavalry
officer and a Russian nobleman. We slid past one another
on the steps. I jalous'd that the World-Conqueror could
not receive one without receiving the others, and so he
received none. We passed the time bribing one another's
servants, way-laying mail and making representations
against the other fellows.

The Shah's chief minister was named Attemadouleh,
who had one foot in the grave and wished to exercise the
other while he still had the use of it. I only understood that
Attemadouleh was not his name but a title, Trust of the
State, when one morning I took my place in the council-
hall to find a different chap seated in the alcove at the
head. The adjoint was excellent company. His principal
demand was that the French Company of the Indies or
His Very Christian Majesty (they not being distinct in his
reasoning) lay down, arm and man a fleet of warships, at
the World-Conqueror's expense, so that he might chastise
the Sultan of Muscate. Since neither side of the bargane
had the smallest chance of being fulfill'd, I consented
with grace. I presume that Captain Watson and Prince
Dolgorukie did likewise.

What occupied me was Father O'Crean's jewel. The
treasure of Delhi, which was housed at the shrine, had

drawn jewellers from the Caucasus, Armenia, Constanti-
nople and Venice. I kept my cards tight against my shirt,
and so did they, but I did hear them speak of an old
polisher at Isfahan, who had known Mr Tavernier back in
Great King Louis's reign, and might or might not still be
alive. Since the amenities of Mashhad were not so great as
to cause me pain in leaving them, I asked Attemadouleh's
permission to visit the former capital, still lying in ruins
after its sack by the Afghans in the year '22. He gave me
an escort which turned back after a league. Not knowing
where I might find water, I tagged a caravan of pilgrims,
returning in high spirits from the shrine, and learned
much of the Persian religion of which the travellers were
greatly fond.

After deposing our bales at the caravansérail, we lodged
all together at the Friday mosque, a fine old building
now much dilapidated, where I followed my companions
in their ablutions and prayers.

The place swarmed with young scholars, of most subtle
reasoning. I told the lads that the King of France, my
master, though himself the most devout of Catholics, had
sent trusted officers to enquire into the doctrine and practice of Islam. While I had been detached to the Guarded
Realms, other gentlemen had gone to the Porte, to Tunis,
to Cairo and to Fez. It proved an excellent stratagem, for

the scholars took their shots not at my religion but the childish errors and disgustful personal habits of the Arab and the Turk. I had not known up to then that at Cairo fathers prostitute their daughters, and that it is the practice of the Turk to shite upright. When the talk became hot, I hosed it with a couplet of Sadi. For a place of worship, the Congregational Mosque of Isfahan is quite merry. In the mornings, I took about my pencil and drawing-book, copied arches and squinks before a carping public, moving daily closer to the Lane of the Gem-Cutters.

I bided my time until the Persian Sabbath, which falls on a Friday by our calendar, when the bazar would be as empty as it would ever be. The jeweller's house was a crazy thing with an outside stair. The cutter, who went by the name Mahmoud, was an old man, with his hair and beard in tangles and his robe patched. He was seated cross-legged on a raised bench, his work-irons about him, in the light of a broad window without glass. I knelt down and placed the pocket on the bench before him and opened the string. He glanced at it and then turned back to his window. After a while, I heard the shuffle of feet in the dust of men returning from divine service.

Never in my life has time passed so slow. Through the window, the air turned blue, then pink then black. I would have exchanged the jewel for a pipe of tobacco. From the gloom, I heard a voice.

"There is within this piece of earth a perfect diamond of four-hundred-and-ninety of your carats weight. It is now New Year. If you return at Harvest, you will find that jewel awaiting you. If I am not living, my son will give it you."

It had been my intention to oversee the cutting, bunking down with my pistols in the shop, but I saw that the scheme would not go.

"May your eye be bright, Master."

"Is the stone for your King, God curse him?"

"For one of them."

"For what purpose?"

"For the front of His Majesty's coronation crown."

"Have you the book of Tavana, may he burn in Hell?"

I drew out from my saddle-bag Mr Tavernier's *Voyages*, and laid it on the counter open at the figure of the great jewels of India. Master Mahmoud let his finger play above the page. Then, without touching the book, he pointed down at a cut with a facet and rounded corners.

"As you command, Master."

XXIX

The return convoi was slow to assemble and, on reaching Mashhad, I found there had been motions at Court. Some fifteen years before, in the turbulency of that age, Tsar Peter of Russia had invaded Persia from the north. After causing some nuisance, his army had returned but had left behind, at a place called Astarabad on an arm of the Caspian Lake, a garrison. The World-Conqueror had gathered a force to march on Khiva and, rather than leave the Russian fortress in his rear, had ordered Attemadouleh to lay the place under siege and bring the dogs of Russians blinded to the capital. I could see that the Attemadouleh had no especial relish for the work, while I had an opportunity to win his favour and the treaty. I proposed to take the fort and hold it for his arrival. I asked for six hundred men and four ten-inch cannon. I received ninety-six men and two of the camel-guns they call zamburak or little wasps.

Where they failed in quantity, my men made up in quality. They could march forty miles in a day on an empty belly and laugh at sundown. They knew no drill but were so intelligent I had only to explain a manoeuvre for them to enact it. They cherised their fire-arms and shot true. They touched no strong waters.

If they had a fault, it was that they did not care for orders. Indeed, the very speaking of a command they held to be irrefutable evidence of ill-breeding. I might make a request, which they might fulfil but only in the manner that they thought righteous. My general staff had a various constitution, sometimes the whole troop, sometimes nobody. Of this group, I selected as my adjutant the most regular in his attendance, Ebrahim Agha, and an adjunct, Mirza Mohsen, to serve when Mr Ebrahim was sleeping or was otherwise disinclined to attend.

"Where are the guns, Mr Ebrahim?"

"We left them on the road. They were heavy."

"How, Mr Ebrahim, shall we now batter a breach in the Russian wall?"

"We shall find a weak place."

That sentiment was approved, while I was held a novice in siege warfare.

Some two leagues before Astarabad, I proposed a halt and the sending out of two parties of scouts. By sun-down of the next day, the men had not returned. On inspecting the camp, I found my strength had melted like snow in the sunshine. I caught Mirza Mohsen assembling a team of asses.

I said: "You are not to go over the rooves to disturb the women and girls. And no thieving."

"Why?"

"All right, some pillage, but no insult to the woman-kind."

I made my own way, through twilight and unattended, to the fort. It was a poor thing, built of mud and clay baked in the sun, with cracks that yawned in the walls and battlements washed down by rain. The ground before the walls, which should have been cleared to give the defence an open field-of-fire, was crowded with the tents of some wandering people. In the moonlight, I could see figures flitting between the crenells.

At the main gate, which was half-open, I found Ebrahim Agha directing several men, bent past the double under booty.

"I need twenty men to disarm the garrison, Mr Ebrahim."

"Why? They will cause a commotion."

"Even so, Mr Ebrahim, we must disarm the guard."

Expecting a dozen, I received the whole troop. We crowded into the guard-house, gathered up the stacked muskets, clothes, caps and cooking tools, bade the sleepy Russians good morning, and crowded out again. I left six men on guard, who soon abandoned their charge to follow me.

The officers' quarter was a wooden building with an

outside stair. Bidding the men wait at the foot, I sprang up and opened the first door. By the night-light, I saw a bed with shapes in it and then a head sprang up, and a neck of ivory and hair like a fountain of gold. My men gasped. The lady threw herself across her husband's body.

"You are not in the smallest danger, madame. I am a French officer, detached into the service of His Majesty the Shah, and these men are the flower of Persian chivalry."

Without turning, I said: "Each night, gentlemen, angels descend from heaven to dance with the Tsar and his officers and attend them to their rest. I have heard of that miracle but never thought myself to witness it."

My men were frozen like statues.

"If, my lady, you give me your parole, I shall take myself and my men away, and wait on your pleasure."

"Never!"

From beneath her came a chiding in Russian. A gentleman's head appeared.

"You have our parole."

"Against my will!"

I turned to the men.

"Gentlemen, we must leave the company to dress and make ready."

"Why? She will fly back to Paradise."

"She has promised me to stay."

The men looked at me in wonder at my credit amid the angelic orders.

XXX

The next morning I called on the Russian commander. His lady was sewing in the corner, while a boy and a girl read at the feet of that feminine officer the Persians call naneh and the English governess.

"Count Bielke . . ."

"Please call me by name."

"Pavel Nikolaevich, I must tell you that I spun a little more yarn last night than I should have done. I ask your pardon and that of your lady."

"I heard you. I was by no means the last in the Oriental Languages examination at the Military Academy. I am glad that your men also recognise that Lidia Petrovna is an angel."

"Oh, nonsense, husband!"

"My men do not for a moment believe it but they do not exclude it and, meanwhile, it spreads a ghostly glamour over their lives. It is better than brandy."

"Really, Mr Neilson, these Persians are the most singular race and I shall be sad to leave them. May I ask, on the strength of our short acquaintance and the great esteem I have for you, that you report my demise to Her Majesty the Tsaritsa? You may spare Her Majesty the particulars."

I had heard Russians were brave, but here was valiance from the heroic age. I had never seen such fair conduct. As for Lidia Petrovna, I did not think for a moment that she would bow her head and stap with her children into Attemadouleh's zenanah.

"I am at your service, Pavel Nikolaevich. I hope none shall be needed. I have a plan that may yet preserve you for Her Tsarian Majesty. Alas! It requires further sacrifice on the part of Mme la comtesse and your children."

That lady looked up from her work. "Nothing dishonourable, I hope, Mr Neilson."

"No, madame. I wondered if you had some jewels of which you are not fond or which are not of the newest fashion."

"All my jewels belong to the one or t'other class."

"If you would select some of lesser value, and particularly those of a devotional character, would you hold them ready for the Attemadouleh's arrival?"

I turned to the children. The little girl smiled at me, but the boy turned away. The agony that his father hid the lad wore on his face for all to see. I said: "Years from now, Sergei Pavlovich, will you try to think less harshly of me?"

Much of the force was busy in taking off the booty out of sight, while I set those I could muster to blow, with the Russian ordnance, a breach in the wall and thereon erect a triumphal arch.

"Mr Ebrahim, you are to leave Attemadouleh sufficient of the spoil to satisfy him."

"He has six piece of cannon."

"And the other weapons and stores and the paychest, if you please, Mr Ebrahim."

He was making calculations in his quick head. "Will you not take something, Mr Vil?"

"I rather like the flags."

"Why do you wish flags?"

"I collect them as mementos of my life."

XXXI

Having no hall of commensurate dignity in the fort, I had resolved that Attemadouleh should be received in the open air. With the help of the wandering people, nimble weavers of the Turkish nation, I had raised before the triumphal arch a sort of canopy open to the winds on four sides and spread with gay carpets. Before it was a triumphal way, lined by the captured cannon and military stores, and the sheep, camels and other hoof-stock that Ebrahim Agha judg'd not worthy his attention.

We heard Attemadouleh a good hour before we saw his dust. He rode down the *via triumphalis* without so much as a glance at his new property. Dismounting with difficulty, he was encumbered with basins, fruits and cordials. With a glare, he shooed them away and stepped onto the carpet. His orator stood just off the carpet behind his left shoulder, while I took the counter position on the diagonall.

Pavel Nikolaevich was led in, hands bound, in his shirt. Behind came the Master of Wrath, or executioner, spade-bearded, dressed head-to-feet in red, and holding a curved sword not unlike our sabre. Pavel Nikolaevich was made to kneel, and his head pressed down upon a leather mat stiff with dried blood.

There was a commotion at the head of the tent. Countess Lidia Petrovna entered. She was dressed in a shift of sack-cloth, which showed to advantage her shape, her feet unshod, ashes on her hair and face, and a hempen halter round her neck. The boy and girl, similarly garbed, noosed and daubed, tip-taed behind her. My men burst into tears. Lidia Petrovna kneeled and taking from her daughter a casket, placed it at Attemadouleh's feet. I went down on one knee, so as to translate her speech.

"Faith of the State and Great Breastplate of the Sultan, we are come to the end of our lives. Before us, the earth gapes and we feel on our faces the flames of Hell and the wafted scents of Paradise. We are the defeated, your prisoners and your slaves. If it is your will to punish our Lord, then we ask in God's name this grace: that we, too, may share his fate, for our bread will have no savour and beds no repose when our Lord's place is empty."

Lidia Petrovna opened the casket, which sent forth a dreary gleam. From my kneeling posture, I could see a gold cross, encrusted in knobby spinels, from the time of Boris Godunov, an icon of Saint Margaret worked in amber, and an embalmed toe in a case of rock crystal and discoloured pearls. It was a treasure more apt to please the antiquary than the lady of fashion, and certain to revolt a Mussulmane gentleman. I dared not turn about, but I was sure my men were of a terrible aspect. Attemadouleh steamed for a while. He made as if to touch the casket with his foot, but better bethought, which was prudent, for my troop would have barked him. Then, evidently deciding to make the best of a bad hand, he said:

"Truly God loves the merciful. You are to leave the sacred land of Iran. If, with God's help, you reach your homeland, you are to tell the Queen of Rus that Attema-douleh made her this gift in pity." The Master of Wrath tutted, made as if to remonstrate, then bowed, lowered his blade and withdrew.

We had been ready for a week and departed Astarabad within the hour. At the head of the column rode Pavel Nikolaevich, with his staff, then the Russian troop, with their matches lit, and drawing one cannon. There followed a litter with the children and Mme Schmutz, lying on the Russian standards. Then came my men in a knot around the litter of Lidia Petrovna. I made the rear-guard.

No Merovingian princess journeyed in such state through olden France. Because of the heat, Lidia Petrovna did not care to close her curtains. We passed through three villages where my soldiers ran about, beating the idling men till they turned their faces to the wall. At our camp that night in an orchard of pomegranates, they erected a tent and a broad enclosure of painted linen screens so that their idol might take the evening air unobserved. The rest of us slept in manure.

On the march next morning, before the heat got up, I heard Lidia Petrovna give an order. The litter slipped behind and came level with me. The curtains opened.

"Do you like money, Mr Neilson?"

"I never had any."

"What do you like, Mr Neilson?"

"I like His Excellency and I like you, Countess."

"And we like you, Mr Neilson. Why, then, are you sad?"

"Am I sad?"

"You seem so."

"My life is not of great purpose, Countess. I fight battles and kill men who are not my enemies, though, thank God, not in this place. I have no wife, no child, no mistress, no friend. I serve the King of France, whom I have never seen and for whom I care not a berry."

"Come to Deer's Glade! His Excellency thinks the world of you. We shall be your friends."

"Thank you, Countess. I cannot."

"Is there a lady in the case?"

"No."

"Tell the truth, Mr Neilson."

"When I was young, at Paris, I loved a young girl and she loved me. I was some years in prison, and in that time she changed her mind, as was her right. When I saw her later, she treated me coldly and sent me away."

"If she has changed her mind once, she will change it again. Do not give up hope, Mr Neilson, or you will die. Do not give up hope."

There was a sort of grumble ahead of us.

"Excuse me, Captain Neilson, my lovers are jealous and shall kill you more swiftly."

I fell back and the litter was again surrounded.

At the river Araxes or Aras, which marked the frontier of the His Majesty the Shah's conquests, there was a ferry-boat and a cable. Pavel Nikolaevich and his children crossed first, and then the Russian soldiers with their horses and the single cannon. Countess Lidia Petrovna was set down. I formed the men into ranks, which just as soon broke up.

"Kindly translate my discourse, Captain Neilson, without your usual augmentations and diminutions."

Countess Lidia Petrovna spoke up: "My lord and I are leaving for the snows. There, under cloudy and brief days, we shall live out the time allotted us. We take with us the memory of your dear faces. Know that, in the years that come, should your sons weary you or your heads ache for a different sky, you have but to inquire the road to Deer's Glade where you shall find bread and salt, and a roof about your heads, and a place to say your prayers. May God protect you all."

We watched Countess Bielke cross and land upon the other side.

XXXII

We had marched but a quarter-league when I saw the men had stopped. A man threw down his musket and sat down. He whispered: "I have seen the limits of the earth and have nothing to report." Another dropped to the ground, and then another, till the whole force was seated on the road, looking out across the treeless plain at their receding souls. I had seen armies break from fear, fatigue, hunger, disease, mistreatment and want of pay but never before from metaphysics.

"Come now, gentlemen," I said. "Are we not Muslims and yet we fall into despair? The lady has left with me a present for you so you shall not forget her. Will you not see her present before you pack your bundles for eternity?"

I drew out the Countess' roubles and made a golden hill on my cloak.

Not a man stirred.

"The lady thought as much and has instructed me that if you will not take the gold, I am to pass it to Attemadou-leh for distribution in alms."

That was effective. The men came up, one by one. Each took a coin, kissed it and placed it in his tunic. There were four rounds until there was but a handful of coins remaining on the cloth.

"Gentlemen, shall we not leave the last ten or twelve pieces as the share of the poor?"

That was approved.

There were groans and cries from the ranks, but no more halts.

The reserved booty was hidden in a thicket of oak woods, or, as we call it in Iran, jangal. Once it was loaded, I stood apart to inspect the column. At the rear came a train of led horses, equipped on each side with a panier holding something wriggling and gay.

"Mr Ebrahim, I expressed my clear intentions about the women in the fort. You have not taken my wishes into account."

"Why, Mr Vil? Because of our valour, they fell in love with us and showed their faces. What were we to do? To preserve the ladies' honour, we had to marry them."

"I see. Very good, Mr Ebrahim. Carry on."

The men had seen an angel, had more gold, horses and wives than they had ever had or would ever have in their lives. Yet they were unhappy. The détour for the spoils, and the moon-faced beauties, had used up our supply. At sundown, the men made their bread from barley-flour and thought themselves ill-used. I sent out hunting-parties, which came back with a pair of pertridge, or an old gazelle, or nothing at all. We passed through two villages reeking with the pelts and carcasses of dead sheep and goats, broken orchards, stripped vines, doors on a hang. Attemadouleh had taken everything. In the second village, an old man lay dead atop his debowelled cow. Ebrahim Agha swore a terrible oath.

On the fifth day, we came on Attemadouleh's track. Across the plain, there was a swath of twenty or thirty feet in breadth, made by the litters holding the cannon. In half a day, we would be on them. I halted and the men surrounded me.

I said: "I propose we send a party with the poor gold and buy provisions from Attemadouleh. After all, it is we that are the poor."

Ebrahim Agha hissed.

"Very well, gentlemen, what is your proposal?"

"Fall on them and kill them and take what is ours."

"I understand, gentlemen. You are good soldiers and will easily prevail. What then? The World-Conqueror will send a force to punish you."

"We shall defeat that, too!"

"Then, my brave soldiers, you must decide which of you is to rule the Guarded Realms. That shall not be easy."

The men were silent. Each thought he would make an admirable Shah. Some demolished the bazar for an enlarged women's quarter; others crucified heretics; while a third part, ambitious to erect a perfect police, burned extortioning bakers in their own bread-ovens.

"You shall be Shah!" There was a roar of acclamation.

"Alas, gentlemen, the King of France my master did not send me to Iran to govern her people but to befriend them for all the ages. If you decide for war, I cannot accompany you. I shall now go apart a distance, so you may debate this matter more freely amang yourselves."

I walked away to a little hillock, of the kind called a teppe, and, once out of sight of the men, smoked a delicious pipe, and then another, somewhat less savourous. After a time, I saw the poneys being relieved of their virtuous burdens. The men had chosen the path of peaceful commerce.

As we approached the capital, our ranks began to thin, and by the time we came to the citadel, I was barely attended. Before the palace vault, there stood the Russian cannon, lying any gate, some off their carriages already well-supped-on by ants. Attemadouleh wanted, it appeared, no tint of a servant's triumph. Beside the guns was a hill of steaming cadavres. Such last in Persia are not, I regret to say, difficult to procure.

Only Mirza Mohsen bade me farewell.

He said: "When you first came, Mr Vil, we thought

you would be tiresome. You have improved. We have made a human being of you."

"May I be your sacrifice, Mirza Mohsen."

"I beg you, not. May I be your sacrifice."

XXXIII

Dressed in tatters like a pauper, smarting from occult and mortal wounds, Attemadouleh was in capital humour. Beside him on the carpet were two copies of the treaty of friendship. I saw that the French side of the treaty was bare of cachets when weighed against those of the Persian side. I had some agates cut into seals in the bazar. Among them were the arms and motto of my mother's family, Hope of Craighall: *At Spes Infracta*, And hope is unbroken, or, as the cutter had it, *at ʒpeʒ infarcta*. I doubt that somewhere in the vaults of the Ministry of Foreign Affairs at Paris, or in the cabinet of some learned Persian, there may be a specimen of my treaty which had not the smallest influence on the politics of the eighteenth century. I thought it prudent to take my leave before the World-Conqueror returned.

Attemadouleh gave me an escort on my way, but after

a while the men began to smell their wives' cookery, and I went on alone. Having ridden the way before, I kept out of the sight of the returning pilgrims, and slept under stupendous stars. I rode under the main gate of the bazar of Isfahan just as the evening prayer was being called, and the merchants were putting up bars across their shops. As I shuffled through the labyrinth, the light became brilliant, rather as, on a fine day, when one comes within three or four miles of the sea. The Gemcutters' Lane was shaking with light. Dazzled, I dismounted to wait out the prayer.

Every now and then, a little boy brought me a note from the market inspectors or muhtasibs, with Draconian fines: ten shahis for riding on horseback in the bazar, fifteen for carrying a fire-arm, and twenty for failing the evening prayer. I shook out some coins for the laddies, with their pots of wine. One of them crept up the steps and then, shading his eyes, and like a commander ordering a general advance, waved his arm.

Master Mahmoud was seated in his place, staring into the unseen. On the bench before him, the stone poured cataracts of light. Beside it were two dishes of blue, unfired clay: the one with the clips, the other with the dust.

"May your hand not give you pain, master."

"May your head not give you pain."

"Will you not sign the jewel for His Majesty?"

"I have done so."

He passed me his glass. I picked it up in my cloak so I should not touch it. At the foot of one face, in script so minute it could not be seen without the glass, was this: The dog of the threshold of Ali, Master Mahmoud his work; and the year 1153 by the Mussulmane calendar. With a complete certainty, I saw why Father Patrick had returned to the Indies. He was seeking the very man that I had found. Without knowing it, I had achieved the first part of my charge. I said:

"Will you not take the dust and clips for your fee, master?"

"Why? Having given up the perfect part, why should I trouble with the imperfect?"

"Because, Master, the clips and dust are worth a very great deal of money. May I do you any service, Master Mahmoud?"

"You will take from me this light that wounds me."

PART 6

Bengal, 1743

XXXIV

There are no carriage-roads in Persia, or any wheeled traffic, so I rode from town to town, by camel, poney or ass, recording the distances, marking wells and sketching forts and caravanseras. I had been three years on my embassy and saw no cause to hurry to India. At Bunder Abbas, I found a boat taking sweet dates to Surate. There I found that war had broken out again in Europe.

The English in India seemed to have no burning wish to fight us, nor we them. His Highness the Nawab of Tanjore summoned me from Pondicherry. He commanded that he had been informed that there was war between the Kings of France and of England; but that since the sea-ports of Hindoustan belonged to His Sovereign Majesty the Great Moghol, it was not proper that foreigners should have bickers and quarrels there. As a precautionary,

Governor Dupleix ordered me to make a survey of the fortifications of both Pondicherry and Karikal, an old town some twenty-five leagues to the south which Mr Du Mas had bought from the Nawab, along with its dependent villages, in '39.

While I was so engaged, word reached the governor that an English squadron, under the command of Mr Barnett, a most capable officer, had taken as prise our company ship, the *Favori* of two hundred tons, off Acheh in the Straits and was now cruising off the Fryar's Hood station eastwards of the isle of Ceylan. Our merchants were in a state of anxiety. Some of the officers were for making a diversionary by falling on the English factory of Saint-David, where a great deal of cloth was baled, but Mr Dupleix was of an opposed opinion. He resolved that, until there should be reinforcement from the metropolis or the islands, or the north-east mousson drive the English squadron into shelter, I should make a strong representation to His Highness the Nawab.

At Arcote, I submitted to His Highness that the English, having by their policy set all Europe aflame, were not unwilling that some of the sparks should take in these parts. I reported on the affair of the *Favori*, which Mr Barnett had added to his strength, and warned that the trade of the Moghol's subject was at equal or greater risk from the English pirates. My eloquence may have weighed less in the balance than the present of twenty-two and one-half aunes of cloth of gold, a fine Arabian horse and three thousand gold pagodas. His Highness graciously said that he would write to the English governor at Madras and Mr Dupleix at Pondicherry with the tauquid that no hostility be committed by men-of-war of either nation in the ports belonging to the Great Moghol or along the sea coast on pain of the destruction of all of that nation's factorys.

After requesting my leave, I was resting my men and horses at noon in the garden of a tumbledown choultrie or temple inn, when something knocked me off my feet. I found myself chest-deep in a wicked-smelling green liquid. About me were the perpendicular walls of the temple tank. From above I could hear a lively fire, and my men withdrawing in good order. I was bris'd and bleeding at the hip from a spent musket-ball.

"Holloa! Hark holloa!"

I looked up and saw a young man peering over the parapet.

"Good day to you, sir. I am, or better was, Captain Neilson."

"Lieutenant Harris. You're not, you know, are you, French?"

"Yes." I thought it better to keep the affair simple.

"The enemy?"

"Yes."

He fumbled his pistol.

"Where are your men, Mr Harris?"

"I don't rightly know."

"Attend to your men and then come back and take me prisoner. As you see, I cannot move. Oh, and Mr Harris . . ."

He did a half-turn.

"Would you kindly bring a rope?"

A lifetime passed before Mr Harris returned, with a squad of men. After many casts, a rope landed in my reach, and I was dragged up to the *terra firma*. Muskets bristled about me. My legs were a congress of leeches.

"Mr Harris, you would oblige me if you would help remove the animals from my legs. Have you a match?"

He was swooning. I said: "Perhaps later."

One of the men passed me the match from his firelock, and I smoaked the creatures off.

As we approached the English camp, I said:

"Mr Harris, I believe you should disarm me."

"Sorry."

He took my proffered sword.

"I have pistols also."

Lieutenant Harris tried to take those but having, like all men, but two hands, he dropped my sword.

"Perhaps if I carry my sword, reversed, as you see, and you carry the pistols, we shall do all right."

"Sir, my French is bad."

"Let us speak good old English."

The English had erected their general-quarter in one of the Nawab's hunting-houses or plesances. I came into a group of officers with, among them, a private man who appeared to be their commander. They had brought in some European furniture which squabbled with the niches and arcades.

The civilian burst out in laughter. He said:

"Not since Paris dropped Achilles with a quirk . . ."

"It is no shame to me, sir, to give my sword to so gallant an officer as Lieutenant Harris."

"Mr Neilson, you are holding your sword."

"Mr Harris was kind enough to return it to me on my parole."

There was more laughter, but without mirth.

I said: "His Highness will not be pleased that the English trading company has, by an act of war, violated the neutrality of his government."

One of the military officers spoke. "It was no act of war

but of criminal police. It appears, Mr Neilson, that you have not grasped the gravity of your position. Now, sir, were you to give us an account of the strength and dispositions of the fort at Pondicherry . . ."

I spun on Mr Harris. "Sir, when I offered you my sword, it was in the confidence that I would be treated according to the laws of war. You have sorely misled me."

Mr Harris opened his mouth, but an officer forestalled him:

"Runagadoes receive no privileges of war, damn-me."

"Steady on, fellows."

"Forgive me, Mr Harris. I was wrong to doubt you. At least one man in the English army has a shred of honour."

There was a roar and glitter of metal.

"Would you release me from my parole, Mr Harris, so I may defend myself?"

"Come now, gentlemen," the official said. "We do not need a browlery. Mr Neilson, you shall go as prisoner-of-war to Saint-George, and take ship thence to face justice in London. And," he said, turning his face away, "since you are such friends, Mr Harris shall command your escort."

The gentleman saw his error, but too late. I said: "I do not know, sir, the practices of the armies of Great Britain.

In our service, no officer takes a command from his subordinate. We shall wait on Captain Harris' brevet."

The official's face turned black and, then, just as soon, beamed as if to say: I see you have learned some wit in France.

"During that time, you will naturally permit me to visit my wounded."

"There are none," somebody said. "They ran away."

We rode out an hour or less before sunset.

"Sit up, Mr Harris. A smart trot. We may ramble once we're in the fields."

Once we had passed the gardens, my companion spoke up.

"Am I truly captain?"

"No. You must earn that rank, Mr Harris, which you may do, first, by finding a match for my pipe."

"Should I smoke, Mr Neilson?"

"Perhaps so. In a soldier's life, there are long periods of inaction. It helps to have something to do."

In the tropicks, the twilight is brief. I was looking for a place for our camp. I was not wholly sure that the English officers had finished with me. Mr Harris followed my gaze.

"What about that hillocky thing yonder?"

"It is your decision, Mr Harris, but I would have chosen so."

"Should I post pickets? There may be, don't you know, Mahrattas?"

"I think it would be wise to have your men used to doing that."

XXXV

From my place of capture to Madraspatnam, where the English had erected their factory of Fort Saint-Georges, I thought it about ninety French miles. Having no relay of horses, we plodded. Mr Harris was the best of company. He began dropping little words of French into his discourse and, by the second day of our ride, we were cracking like attorneys in the Salle des pas-perdus at Paris. I suspected that a congenial diffidence, and the incessant bullying of his brother-officers, had all but extinguished in my companion a lively intelligence.

"I am not a Jacobite, Mr Harris. Indeed, I hold the Jacks for a parcel of fools."

Mr Harris pulled in his mount. "Do you mean that . . . I mean that . . . Is there a . . .?"

"You can say it, Mr Harris."

"Is there a . . . You know. A person . . .?"

"Do you mean a lady?"

"Mmmmm."

"No."

There was a jeering and gaffawing from the men. In a garden beside the road, Cavalryman Cade, on his knees in his sleeves, was planting onions, while a lady chittered at him from the shade of a palm, her wrapper across half her face.

"Some offence against military discipline, Mr Harris?"

"In the night, Cade stole a chicken from the widow. Perhaps, too lenient?"

"Not at all."

"Too severe?"

"No. Exactly right, Mr Harris."

Once the fort of Saint-George was in sight, Mr Harris became taciturn. He reined in and said:

"You won't, you know, look, will you, Captain Neilson?"

"No, Captain Harris, for I have given my parole. But you shall."

We stared as one at the Fort's miserable state of defence. It appeared that the English merchants were as niggard as our own. From the land side, the courtine wall, to a length of about fifty toises, was ruinous while to the north the town of Madraspatnam straggled so close that one might advance a mortar to within ten feet of the fort. Before us was a sort of meadow where three bony beeves jostled for a single blade of grass with but a bare-feet girl to guard them and a hangar, which I took to be the powder store, with no guard at all.

"Why are there two church steeples, Mr Harris?"

Mr Harris sulked. "There are as many Papists in the town as Anglicans."

"Ah. I had not known that."

"What does it matter? Nobody hears me."

"They shall, Mr Harris. They shall."

Mr Harris put his horse into a trot while I looked resentful and distrait. As we pattered onto the parade, and grooms rose from their mats under the trees, I saw a knot of English officers clapping their sides in merriment. We dismounted and made our way towards the guard-house. One of the English officers was behind me and, a moment later, I was sprawled amid the sand and dung.

Mr Harris had his sword drawn.

"Mr Harris! You do not draw sword on a brother officer!"

"Cudlipp tripped you. I saw him."

"Even so, Mr Harris."

Mr Cudlipp and his friends were walking backwards as one does, having stepped on a serpent's nest.

"Go now, at once, sir, to Mr Cudlipp before the other fellows wind him up like a clock. Better, I shall go as your witness."

Captain Harris looked serious.

"Mr Harris, you are not in danger. There is not the slightest chance that you shall be injured. My fear is that poor Mr Cudlipp might come to harm."

XXXVI

Mr Browne, Mr Cudlipp's witness, was old and red to be a captain.

"Une mauvaise affaire . . ."

"Would you not prefer to speak in English, sir?"

"A deuc'd bad business."

"Mr Harris accepts fault and apologises without reservation. He is prepared both to submit to military justice and to offer Mr Cudlipp satisfaction."

Mr Browne was startled by the surrender. "Well, sir, I do not think we need to go to martial law. What do you think?"

"Sir, remember I am an enemy and Mr Harris' prisoner. If it were up to me, I would propose a single exchange of shots at dawn tomorrow on the sea shore. I have a pair of pistols, made at Paris and lately given me by Mr Dupleix, which I would like you to examine."

If Mr Browne had hoped for some secluded spot, a Leith Sands or Scheveningen, he was deceived. Already, with dawn scarcely broke above the sea-line, fishermen had landed their catch and were marketing the fish from temporarie buiths. As the duelling party moved off, so the fish-market followed and with it an agglomeration of spectators. Since one spot was much like ane other, I proposed to Mr Browne that the fight proceed before this publicum. The spray from the breakers, turned to vapour by the heat, made the place like a Persian bath.

Mr Harris was in the best of moods, Mr Cudlipp less so.

"What's Harrisy so happy about?"

"Eh, Mr Cudlipp? Shall we have this over and done? Then one of us, at least, can breakfast. Ha-ha."

"Mr Harris!" I said. "I remind you that you are engaged in an affair of honour in which you have owned fault. I would wish you to temper your high spirits."

"Sorry. Mum's the word."

Having seemed merely preoccupied, Mr Cudlipp now looked queersome. He had made the mistake of wearing his spurs, which tinkled over the *basso continuo* of the breakers.

"Mr Cudlipp!" I said. "When I speak the word 'Present', Mr Harris will receive your shot."

That officer stood square-on, and stifled an early-morning yawn.

"Ladies!" I cried in jargon. "Will you kindly take your children out of the line of fire?"

There was a cuffing and a calling. After some minutes, we had a raggedy space.

"Make ready, gentlemen. Mr Cudlipp! Present!"

There was a splutter of powder. Had Captain Cudlipp shot straight, I doubt he would have done much hurt. As it happened, he missed.

Mr Harris raised his pistol at Mr Cudlipp's head.

I whispered: "Don't you dare, Edmund Harris!"

The spell broke. With a quick motion, Mr Harris puffled a shot above his head.

There was a murmuring among the English officers.

One said: "We think you tampered with the powders."

I leered at them. "If you believe that, gentlemen, you should address yourselves to Mr Browne. If he asks for a second shot, I shall agree to it. Mr Harris, as the gentleman at fault, deloped. If there is a second shot, he may elect to shoot to wound. If, however, Captain Harris falls, my parole lapses and I shall fight you not as a gentleman but as an enemy and with all the greater ferocity in that you have impugned my honour."

While that was sinking in, I called out: "Come now,

gentlemen, shall we not breakfast here on the shore. Let us have bread and fried fish and salad greens and the ruby wine of Shiraz and all at the expense of His Very Christian Majesty of France!"

I bespoke those things in jargon and for a while there was an erecting of tables and lighting of fires and displaying, selecting and frying of fish. Little boys scoured the sand for the spent balls. It was merry enough. Our public appeared to be charmed by our European customs, where one moment we are blazing away and at the next linking arms and baying for toasts. Yet the racket did not wholly cover the Englishmen's grudge. They had come to see blood and had seen none. Nobody appreciates a shot fired at heaven. There was no sign of Mr Barnett's squadrone. I thought it prudent soon to take Mr Harris away from Fort Saint-George, and he had the men up and riding out within an hour.

In the fields, Mr Harris turned on me. "You wet the powder."

"I did not, Mr Harris."

"Swear on your lady's life that you did not!"

"I do not have a lady. I have but myself, and I swear on my life."

Captain Harris was at a loss. "Then how the deuce, Mr Neilson, did you know I would come to no harm?"

"Because, Mr Harris, of your insouciance. Captain Cudlipp is not a quarrelsome man, and he felt ashamed of his conduct. He only challenged you to save his countenance before his brothers. The poor man only had to see you so gay to lose his nerve. There was only a bit chance of his hitting you."

"I was only so careless because you made me so. It was not fair on Cudlipp."

"Mr Harris, are you not glad to be alive?"

He gazed about him at cattle and white herrons, and women reaping and smoak from dinner fires and said: "Yes." Then: "Why are you so kind to me, Mr Neilson?"

"Kind? I am not kind to you. Indeed, I must ask your pardon. The day I was taken at the temple, I saw you were not appreciated by your fellows. I was enraged to be a prisoner, and sought to display a superiority to your detractors. The memory of my conduct oppresses me and I ask your forgiveness."

"Because of her?"

"Who?"

"Your lady."

"I have no lady. I told you that."

"Yes, you have, if not on your arm, at least in your breast. Within your heart, you have placed her as a judge, free of the weaknesses of her sex or the confusions of ours, of greed, vanity, ambition, anger, envy and what we in our folly call honour, before whom you lay all your actions and projects for arbitration."

"Too deep for me, Mr Harris."

That officer took a breath of the most perfect contentment. "I shall fight no more duels. They are a foolish physical exercise."

"I am sure you are right." And then: "Do you have money, Mr Harris?"

"No. Do you?"

"No."

"We shall shift somehow, Mr Neilson. How far is it to Calcutta?"

"One thousand English miles."

"Oh," Mr Harris said.

XXXVII

Mr Harris sold his watch, saddle and spurs. I sold Mr Dupleix's pistols. I kept my sword only as the evidence of my parole. The country was crossed with broad rivers and we made many and weary deviations. At the village of Pachipour, for services rendered in dispersing a nest of

Mahratte scouts, an action in which Mr Harris twice exposed himself to fire, I bartered five maunds of Jambousier wheat and an ox and a cart of forage for our horses. When the village men, now in security, regretted their magnificence and contended there had been no bargane, Mr Harris offered to burn down their houses for them.

"Is she at Calcutta?"

"I beg you, Captain Harris, not to play more on that theme. I have said, more than once, I believe, that I have no lady."

"Then why don't you escape? You might have stayed on the far bank of the river with the horses. Or skipped away in the fight with the Pindaries."

"I have given you my word."

Captain Harris fell back, talking to himself.

At Masulipatnam, where Mr Cardoso had a factory for painted cloths, I managed to borrow a pittance on the credit of my industrial friend. With the few coppers, and the promise of our service in any fight, we took passage on a coasting vessel for Calcutta. I had encouraged Mr Harris to keep a journal, and he whiled away the time writing for the Honourable Directors a report on our Odyssey. Since the fight at Pachipour, the men needed little direction. As they lounged and smoked in the shade of the latine sail, the sailors tip-taed around them. By the time we reached Ballasore Road and took on a pilot for the river, we were as jettie as Africans.

It was weary work ascending the river against the stream, and Mr Harris put his men to hauling. Opposite Fort-William, which is the English company's stronghold at Calcutta, amid a tumulte and flotilla of jostling boats, there lay a warship of the greatest force I had ever seen. On my inquiry from our skipper, I learned it was His Majesty's first-rate ship-of-the-line, *Galatea,* mounting seventy-two guns, Captain Baker commanding. Detached from Mr Barnett's squadron, she had come to Calcutta for victual and was being made ready to sail with merchant goods (and, no doubt, a renegade prisoner) for London.

Fort-William was more extensive than Fort Saint-George, and better made of brick and mortar. About the fort was a town perhaps as populous as Paris, but more concentrated. I saw for the first time that England would be a great power in the world, or was already, greater than France, greater than the Moghol dominion, greater even than China. I knew nothing of England. I knew only Mr Bigby and Mr Harris. So be it, I thought. I was taken, without irons, to a room on the first floor of the barrack. I was smoking my pipe on the varanda or balcony over-looking the exercise-ground when Mr Harris came running at me.

"I am for England! With despatches!"

"That is no less than you deserve, Mr Harris. Shall we be shipmates with Mr Baker? I would much like that."

"Alas! Mr Braddille believes we have been too much in each other's company for the good of the King's service. I am to await the coming of Mr Barnett's whole squadron."

"That is my loss, Mr Harris."

He looked uncertain.

"What is it, Mr Harris?"

He had fallen into his old diffidence.

With a struggle, he said: "Would you be so kind as to help me write, you know, a letter?"

"Fie, Mr Harris, you are well capable of writing a letter in French."

"It is not in French."

"I see. Shall you take up your pen?"

He did so.

"Now, what is the lady's name?"

"Charlotte Elizabeth."

"Dear Lottie . . ."

"No."

"Sweet Carlotta?"

"Please not."

"Dear Charlotte?"

Mr Harris looked miserable.

"Dear Miss Charlotte Elizabeth. I write this from Calcutta, a fine town of ours on the river in Bengale, where I am running an errand for Mr Braddille. We had a fight with the French down the coast, where I overpowered the black traitor and renegade ..."

"Steady on!"

"... where I was lucky enough to receive the sword of poor Captain Neilson, who had the misfortune to displease His Majesty, and out of pique, P-I-Q-U-E, took service with the King of France. I am to deliver him to Captain Baker of H.M.S *Galatea* for transportation to London, where he may hope for His Majesty's clemency, but must expect his justice. I am made captain."

Mr Harris's eyes sparkled, as if to say: I can do this. So very hard it is not.

"Now, Mr Harris, some love."

He shuddered. "Please, no love."

"Do you have a rival, Mr Harris?"

"Mr Scuse."

"Mr Scuse?"

"The curate at Langton Parva."

"Sometimes, at Sunday service at the garrison church here, when the monkeys crowd the window-shelves outside to jeer at their Anglican cousins ..."

"Too clever."

". . . Sunday service with my men at Saint-Anne's church outside our fort, I ask Our Lord if I have made a mistake. When I think of the ivy-covered spire . . ."

". . . moss-cloaked tower . . ."

". . . of Langton church and the rooks squabbling in the immemorial elms . . ."

". . . cedars . . ."

". . . and my dear parents and Miss Char . . ."

". . . and my dear parents and good friends . . ."

". . . I wish I had never left the shores of England. Yet here my horizons have receded and, at the price of a few cuts . . ."

". . . a scratch or two . . ."

". . . I have gained an expanded view, some credit and a good estate . . ."

". . . and a competency."

"After handing Mr Neilson . . ."

". . . (not without some small regret, for he is not a truly bad, I mean a deep-dyed, sort of rascal, merely impetuous) . . ."

". . . I am to wait on Mr Braddill and receive his orders for England. I trust it will not displease her if, as soon as I set foot on London ground, straightaway I fly. . ."

"No flying, sir!"

". . . if, having discharged my business at Court and in

the City, I amble down to Surrey to have the honour of calling on Miss Charlotte Elizabeth . . .

" . . . Belcher . . ."

" . . . of . . ."

" . . . Dorking . . ."

" . . . of the fairest land on earth."

He read it over, and then sighed. He said: "It is fine enough. Unfortunately, not a word of it is true."

"It was not true. It is now."

With the appearance of the greatest effort for so small a motion, Mr Harris nodded.

"Now, Captain Harris, you would oblige me if you would have delivered for me a letter less interesting. It is addressed to Mr Jogot Shett, Hindou merchant of this place. As you see, it is not sealed. It concerns money matters."

He glanced at my Nastalique. "I, too, shall learn Persian."

"Nobody ever regretted knowing Persian."

Captain Harris looked at me in a sort of enlightenment. "Tobacco. French. Persian. Persian. French. Tobacco. Is that the sum of it, Mr Neilson?"

"It is more profound than that, Mr Harris, inestimably more profound. Those three are the beginning."

XXXVIII

Mr Braddille, the English India Company's president in the Bay of Bengale and governor of Fort-William, was dictating in Persian to four secretaries. He finished, skimmed the letters of infelicities, and signed them. As the men bowed out, he said:

"I am obliged to you, Captain Neilson, for the great improvement you have wrought in Mr Harris' deportment and efficiency. You saw in him something that we did not see. I shall advertise that to the Court of Directors."

"It was nothing of my doing, sir. Mr Harris needed but a broader field to show his very great promise."

"Mr Harris shall be gazetted captain. Yet I must warn you, Mr Neilson, that matters do not stand well for you in the west end of London. Now if you was to bide a while with me . . ."

"To betray one country, Mr Braddille, might be inadvertence. To betray two looks like bad character. I have long wished to see London. They say it is more populated than Paris."

"For God's sake, William, the Ministry has a great resentment of you since the action at Gingee. Do you want to die in a pool of blood and shite on Tyburn Hill?"

I felt his question did not absolutely require an answer.

"I shall not ask you to bear arms against the King of France. I would wish you by me as my Oriental Secretary. Mr Jogot Shett is cooking up some khichree in Burra Bazar, and has a mind to use me. We shall see who uses whom."

"I am sure."

"Or I would dearly like your help in the Revenue. Mr Harris tells me you were intimate with Mr Law."

"I admired him more than I knew him. Thank you, sir, but I may not."

"Mr Harris says there is a lady in the case."

"There is a lady in Mr Harris' case but none, alas, in mine."

Mr Braddille began to pace. He said: "I never apprehended this thing of ladies. A man sees his duty, his pleasure or his interest. He follows them wheresoever they may lead. If he wishes for feminine company he may pile his zenanah to the rafters. What in the Devil's name have ladies to do with it?"

"I have no idea, Mr Braddille."

He gave up. He said: "Mr Neilson, my officers wish to give a supper for you. They have a notion to have Mr Baker drunk, to the glory of the land service and the confounding of the sea."

"Shall you honour us, Mr Braddille?"

"I shall leave before the songs."

The supper was at a garden in the northern suburbs of the town, managed by a man who called himself Perrin. It was a delicious place. My hosts drank like Germans. After a while, Mr Baker arrived, supported on two sailors. He was dead-drunk, and though my English friends plied him with arrack-punch, nothing they could do could make him more or less so. He summoned me and scorched my ear in a foreign tongue, which I believe he intended to be French.

For all my weakness for strong waters, and most certainly Goa arrack, I saw after a while that Mr Harris and Mr Braddille wished me to escape, which I did, but not without many toasts and embraces and farewells and promises to renew our acquaintance in St James's, where the play runs high and the Champagne deep.

Captain Harris accompanied me through the moonlight to the garden gate. We had turned tables. He stood upright. I was fit to greet like a wean.

I said: "So that your candour towards me give not the least advantage to the King of France, I promise not to bear arms against Great Britain for a period of six months from this day."

"I do not require that, Mr Neilson."

"I shall act thus, none the less."

He said in French: "May I shake your hand, Captain Neilson?"

"With the greatest pleasure, Captain Harris."

A little later I heard him roaring for brandy-pauni.

I made a befuddled way to Mr Jogot Chet's house in Bara Bazar and slept with the petitioners in his courtyard.

XXXIX

Mr Harris, who had that faculty of fellow-feeling more often found in women than in men, had seen into my projects. The reader may remember that Mme la marquise de Maurepas had drawn on Mr Chet in my favour the sum of five hundred gold louis; or rather, she had endossed with her credit a bill for the same from Mr Law of Lauriston that had not a chance of being honoured. I had suffered myself to be led prisoner to Calcutta so that I might cash the bill, not because I wanted money (or wanted money more than on any other day) but to honour Mme la marquise's liberality and open-handedness. It was the only tie to her that remained me. I wished also Mme de Maurepas to know that on that day, April 1, 1745, Captain William Neilson was among the living.

I believed that Mr Chet would not object to me cooling my heels in his outer courtyard, and it was not until long into the afternoon that I was admitted to his dewan-hall. That assembly, as befitted the counting-house of the richest private subject on God's earth, was mean and grimy, lit by high windows without glass, cooled by a single servant with a fann of leaves, and packed as a prison. It took me some time to distinguish my host from the mass of persons, all in white, kneeling on rush mats. I was the most gaily dressed gentleman in the place, which is not a condition I have much known in my life.

In India, public manners are so restrained one might pass a whole life in the country without so much as a jostle. That afternoon, everything about my person was a racket: the King's uniform, my jingling spurs and sword, my spreading hat, my cawing voice and even, Lord knows, my European stink. The gentlemen let their eyes slide away from me as if from the sun. I held out the bill, then dropped it on a tarnished trey, which passed from one gentleman to another and then a third, and a fifth, before coming to rest a little to the front and side of Mr Chet, who glanced at it and looked away.

The man at his right spoke. "Mr Law is dead, a bankrupt."

Bankrupt babbled from every throat.

"No doubt," I boomed. "Yet if the gentleman was to turn the bill over, he shall see that it is endossed by Mme la marquise de Maurepas, lady-governor of the Mascarenian islands."

"Jaan Begum is dead on the pyre of Morpath Sahib, her lord."

Dead dead dead, said the hall.

I stamped my foot. The action, though it arose in fear, appeared as anger. I bellowed:

"Do not dishonour Jogot Sahib with untruths!"

It was untrue. More than that, I could see that every man was thinking that it might be wise, for a crum of peace and quiet, to have me out of there.

"I shall now take my leave and in a month, or two months, Jaan Begum will come in person to inquire why Mr Jogot Chet, merchant of Calcutta, refused to honour her bill."

Mme de Maurepas, in a skirt five yards in the round, pale as ice and blazing like a fire, engulfed the hall like a nightmaire.

Without any order from Mr Chet, or indeed from any person I could see, a half-dozen of servants padded in with piled treys.

"Does Jogot Sahib honour bills in copper! Jaan Begum's

bill particularises gold Louis of Paris at the weight and fineness of that day."

The orator sneered. "Jogot Sahib has no trade with France. Here is money of the country."

"Sir, you have given me made-up tales and now discourtesies. That I did not expect from the servants of Jogot Sahib. Bring me the gold and I shall be gone for ever from among you."

Mr Chet looked at his orator. The orator said:

"Where is the Jogot Khan's jewel?"

I pointed to my chest.

I thought that might have some small effect, but I was not prepared for what happened. Each man rose like a charmed snake. All ties of friendship, caste and subordination had been obliterated and there would be a fight of all against all. The diamond materialised, in a convenient compass, all possibility in this world below of fortune, power, fame, happiness and salvation. I saw that I had been rash to carry the jewel with me, but what was to be done? Had I given it to Mr Harris for safe-keeping, I would have entangled him in an affair of treason to his master, King George.

I said: "Before you kill me, gentlemen, know this. I have left letters with the English, with the request that, should I not return from this house of friends, those letters

should be placed before His Royal Highness the Subah-
dare. His Royal Highness will be justified in asking why
Mr Jogot Chet, a mere subject, wishes to own a jewel
worth five crore of rupees. Might it be that Mr Jogot
Chet has in mind, with or without his English friends, to
make a revolution in Bengale?"

Eyes slid away from the merchant.

I ploughed on. "Mr Crean was my beloved gourou and
I am his heir-at-law. If Mr Jogot Chet regrets his bargain
with Crean Sahib, that is as nothing to me. Mr Jogot
Chet's credit in this world is worth far more than the jewel
but that credit will be as a piece of dung the very moment
a man of you lays a hand on me."

A second servant and a second trey appeared, covered
this time with a painted cloth. I opened my saddle-bag.
The which being filled to the golden brim, I walked out
backwards, in part out of respect for so very opulent a
business man, in part to spare my back from the shock of
a dagger.

I believed Mr Chet would leave me safe until I had
recovered and destroyed the letters. He could not imagine
that they did not exist. In the gloaming, I could hear his
people before and behind me, flittering along the rooves,
or scuttling down lanes. I saw them clagged to walls or
spread on litters in postures of deathly repose. I glided

through the gate of the fort as if it were my own house.

In Mr Harris' room, I left the gold coins on his stool, with the written message: *For the enterprise of Dorking.* On the window-syll, with the grand gestures of a tragic player, I burned some torn and crumbled drafts of my friend's letter to Miss Belcher. By good fortune, I found the washer-man and changed His Very Christian Majesty's uniform for a raggedy gown and clartie turban. In this sordid costume, I passed like a ghost through Mr Chet's servants and out of the famous city of Calcutta.

PART 7

Return to the Metropolis, 1745

XL

I had long been attracted by the personage of the mostoufi, who is a sort of itinerant book-keeper. In that character, I travelled south. I dozed on my heels outside store-houses, or scrawled in minuscule Persian cipher on a reel of paper, which gathered the curious and conferred on me a wizard's glamour. I imagined Mr Law looking down and approving my progress in the mysteries of accounts. Nearly twenty years had elapsed since I had come into India. I had no wishes and no attachments. I might even now be measuring seers of rice and counting head of goats but for the jewel blazing in my shirt.

At Madraspatnam, I skulk'd in what the English call the Black Town. Strung out a mile apart in the rode were the eight sail of Mr Barnett's squadron, including our ship *Favori*, now called *Medway's Prise*. My half-year furlough being almost spent, and anxious that Mr Barnett was preparing to fall on the French establishments, I went on my way.

In a shimmer out in Pondichéri road I thought to see the darling outline of the *Atalante*, and hoped my friend Mr Béranger was in command. My arrival at our general quarter caused merriment. It seemed Mr Braddille had sent an officer under flag of truce with a note to say that in a desperate action I had broken ship and plunged into the Houglie and he feared that I had perished in the attempt. Mr Béranger came in and burst out laughing.

In a private interview, I gave Mr Dupleix a report of my absence and of my word to Mr Harris, for which latter reason I could furnish no military intelligence about the navigation, fortifications and strength at Fort Saint-George, except to say that they would reward a careful reconnaissance.

Among the packets Mr Béranger had brought from the metropolis were, in recognition of my foolish Persian treaty, the blue ribbon and star of the Order of Saint-Louis and the brevet of lieutenant-colonel. My debt to the Company of the Indies, which had increased by the compounding of the semi-annual rent to 2,691,588 livres and six sols, the Directors graciously consented to annul. I was commanded to return to France for the special service of the King. I asked Mr Béranger if I might serve on *Atalante* at my old rank of ensign-lieutenant, but he became vexed, saying that I would thereby abolish the equivalencies between the two services, and I must now deport myself as befitted the second man in the colony, and like soon to be the first. We embarked for the company 1,385 bales of piece goods, as well as two dozen or more bales for private merchants.

"I must warn you, William, that this will be *Atalante*'s last voyage. She is condemned, but if we treat her as she deserves she will bring us dry to old France."

XLI

At the île de France, I learned that Mr Maurepas had died, of a quinsy of the throat, and that his widow, after governing the island with sense and justice for three years while the new governor, Mr Bourdonnais, cavilled at the Navy Department over his appointments, had left with her ladies-in-waiting on the *Triton* bound for Saint-Malo. Mr Bourdonnais himself had sailed away some weeks before me with a ship-of-war of sixty guns and five armed merchantmen, bent on some private enterprise of plunder.

I made no visit to the Government House, lest I lose mastery of my heart. In the churchyard of Port-Louis, I had head-stones cut for poor François Delacour and Father Patrick O'Crean.

Dear Mr Ézéchiel was no more. He was a connoisseor of women and, sailing a little far in that channel, had been stabbed to death by a committee of married men. Thus perished an artist who might have added lustre to any Court of Europe or India. If, as Mme de Maurepas said once, Original Genius may be born in a shed, it may also bleed to death on the dirt floor of a cabaret. Of Mr Durfort, I asked for no word and received none.

What caught my eye was the increase in provisions, and a consequent cheapness. The markets of Port-Louis were heaped with fruits and pasture beef. Father Borthon told me that Mme de Maurepas had bought, from her own fortune, the freedom of some one hundred Africans and given each of them two arpents of land in the back-wood. So long as each cleared his plot within one year, and consented to do one week's service in the corvée or road and harbour works, he might hold the land in simple fief for perpetuity.

The King, ravished at the disposal of his lands by a vassal or not wishing to cross so dangerous a proconsul, confirmed the allotments. The slave-owners, believing they had a rich buyer for the wretched of Madagascar and Mocambique, contracted with the Danish pirates for another ship which came in with its gunwhales in the water and bodies heaped on the deck only to find that the governoress' purse was shut. Pirates, being pirates, have to be paid. In the end, the holders settled with Mme la Marquise at a loss of eighty *per centum*. Mr Bourdonnais, who inclined like Mr Maurepas towards the slave-holding party, halted the grants but was unable to abolish them.

Not all the freedmen made good cultivators and husbandmen, but many did. Among the haggard scarecrows were sturdy African yeomen, delighted to be working for themselves and pleased as Punch to be French. Their ladies and daughters, decked in Indian calicoes, made a sight for the eyes at Sunday service or on the quay thereafter where they sampled Persian sweets while their menfolk trucked predictions on the rains. I doubt that Mme de Maurepas intended that the increase of the free Africans, their greater fecundity and lesser mortality, must in the end so justle or crowd the bonded that slavery in the île de France would end not by decree but by a natural or rather, if I may use so violent an expression, a political oeconomy. I was proud to have served that lady, if only for a little while.

The other consequence, Father Borthon said, was that

skippers of all nations put in at Port-Louis for fresh provisions and water, and one might at any time see five or six vessels in the road. Captains had to tag their sailors and marines lest they desert. As for ourselves, once Mr Béranger had stocked and put up sail, we rioted for a week on salad and pamplemousses while *Atalante* groaned and sighed beneath us.

Among the officers was a lad named Neiret, on his first campaign as volunteer or ensign. He was of a good family of Rennes that, at the sudden death of his father, had fallen on evil times. In as much as I could judge such things, he was an efficient officer who never shirked a task, and was withal as lovely and graceful as a young girl. I feared for him in that nest of sodomites that is the French merchant marine, but the care of Mr Béranger had so far preserved him from insult. Mr Neiret was eager to learn, read books of every sort in his off-watches, and sought out my company each day, for which, in my idleness, I was grateful.

Mr Béranger's anxiety, which the lad communicated to me, was to avoid Mr Bourdonnais, lest we be dragged into some privateering affair for which *Atalante* had neither the youth nor the agility. Believing that active officer to be in the vicinitie of Madagascar, the Captain had the master-pilot steer far to the south of the island. We touched the coast of Africa at the Point of Natal where, Mr Neiret said, the master-pilot hoped to profit from the currents coming from the Canal of Mocambique, and we coasted through fogs, dropping the lead every hour lest we touch on the banks. Though we saw not the shore, the tops of far-away mountains appeared above the fogs. It was slow going, the wind from every quarter, and high seas. Not knowing if the Hollanders had managed to remain neuter, or whether England had press'd the States-General to declare war on France, Mr Béranger made no halt at their Fort, though we had been a full six weeks without supply of fresh vittal. On the day of the New Year, we sang the *Te Deum* to thank Our Lord for giving us the grace to pass the Cape.

Once we had doubled the Cape, we had plain sailing and steady winds from the south-east, which the men hoped might carry us all the distance to the Line. On the best days, we ran six knots of the corde each hour, or more than one hundred miles in a day and night. As once on the *Prince-de-Conty*, I began to look about me. What I saw I did not like. In the midst of a mainoevre, a sailor might sit down or snarl at his brother through a black mouth. I caught a mousse or cabin-lad and, while he wauled and yelped, I rolled up his sleeve on blisters. Legs swelled fit to burst breeks. Some men sat for hours without moving.

Others raved liked madmen. One by one, I watched the poor men of the company fall prey to the disease of scurvy.

Because of our labours in doubling the Cape, and because we had not put in to the Hollanders' settlement, it was now full two months since the men had touched fresh food. By January 9th, there were thirty men down. At noon on the morrow, at the time of taking the altitude, the Captain did not appear on the dunette. During the night following, he vomitted much and was bled white until the surgeon-major, Mr Salbe, himself succumbed. I put a halt to the cupping and ordered that, in place of tisane, Captain Béranger should have wine. To add to our miseries, *Atalante* was shipping water.

I sought out Mr Neiret. I said: "Will you not call all the commissioned officers and the maître to a council? In the Council Chamber?"

Mr Neiret stiffened.

"There, will you not read aloud the Captain's orders? I shall support you in everything you decide, Mr Neiret. Without reservation."

"Shall you attend the Council?"

"No, sir."

A little later, I was summoned to the Council Chamber. Mr Neiret was standing, as if he thought it sacrilege to use the Captain's furniture. The officers looked at him and then at me. All spoke in whispers, so as not to disturb the Captain rolling in his cot behind the screen.

Mr Neiret said: "Captain Béranger's orders are to anchor at the islands of Fernando Noronho, off the Brazils, and there await two of the King's warships to escort us into Lorient rode."

I said: "I do not believe, M. Neiret, that we can win through to Fernando Noronha. I believe that M. Salbe and Père Linnatte, were they in correct health, would advise that the Captain and the sick men should recuperate on shore. I believe, M. Neiret, that you should mark a course for the island of Saint-Helena."

XLII

"What are you doing, Colonel Neilson?"

Mr Neiret caught me red-hand among the Captain's stock-in-trade.

"I am looking out a present for the English governor of Sainte-Hélène."

"That is pillage, M. Neilson."

"As you command, M. Neiret."

A little later, he came to me with ninety aunes of

Patna silk, a commission from the dowager duchesse de Bourbon. That lady, a daughter of the great king, was principal shareholder in the Company of the Indies.

"I have heard Her Royal Highness is a lady of sense. If we survive, shall you write to her in explanation?"

"Yes."

"Well, let us survive then."

"But what will she do to me?"

"She will summon you and place you on the carpet and then forgive you and raise you to great heights."

"We shall survive."

XLIII

At the island, we put up the Swedish pavilion, and I left in the chaloupe with two sailors who knew no French to give Mr Dunbar his present. I said we were Swede merchants, stricken with the scurvy. He did not believe me, but he did not have to believe me. The cloth passed muster. When I asked for news of Europe, Mr Dunbar dismissed me.

We carried the Captain and the sick ashore so they might breathe the land air and touch soil. It was our bad luck that the water was dirty from the rains, and there were no fruits or fresh meat which the men craved. From Saint-Helena, a stern wind carried us to Ascension Island, where the sailors caught three turtles to make bouillon for the sick. The men lay in wait upon the strand, in silence, till the poor creatures, so swift in the sea and clumsy on land, came out of the suffe. In a cleft in the rock, I was shown a wine bottle where the Company captains leave messages one for another. Mr Neiret wrote a letter for the Directors, should matters turn out ill for us. There were now but three sailors to each watch. The almoner, Father Linatte, died. Remembering my duties on the *Prince-de-Conty*, I read the burial service.

On February 2nd, Mr Neiret reduced the water ration to half a Paris pint and the nourishment to a single galette each man. The water, full of little white worms, had to be strained through mousseline. To catch the rain, I had the sail-maker drape cloth that had not been treated with pitch forward of the artimon, weigh it down with ballast from the hold, then pierce a hole with a funnel beneath to catch the rain. When it came in torrents, we collected in an hour eight hogsheads of rain water, clear and without worms, which Mr Neiret had lashed to the side between the cannons, and fastened with paddock-locks.

In the Council Chamber, Mr Neiret was at the point of tears. "I do not have any idea of our longitude."

"It does not matter. Bear north till you feel cold on your face and turn through ninety degrees to the east."

"But we shall miss our escort of warships!"

"We shall have to forgae their company."

"That is in defiance of the Captain's orders!"

"M. Neiret, in writing those orders, the Directors had no notion that at some season of her charmed existence *Atalante* would have forty-five men out of action, and be shipping water at the rate of six feet every twenty-four hours. I believe they would confide in the prudence of the officer commanding that, in cases unprovided for in his instructions, he should act as he thought fit for the welfare of his command and the service of His Majesty and the Company's actioners."

Mr Neiret whispered: "I would like to see my mother again, and my sisters."

"You shall, M. Neiret, and another, who this very time is standing by the wind-mill at Lorient, searching the horizon."

"Who is she, M. Neilson?"

"She scarcely knows herself, or why she walks a Sunday the road to the île de Groix. If anything can bring you home, it is her will."

"How shall I know her, M. Neilson?"

"I wouldn't worry about that."

For those still standing, there was no repose. The great hune mast was rotten, and for the first time in my life, and by God's grace I pray the last, I went up in the shrouds to help the men take it down and put up the reserve. The rudder was splinter'd, and we opened the Sainte-Barbe, the master-gunner's store beneath the Captain's chamber, to replace it.

League by league, *Atalante* was carrying us to safety. We passed the Line on February 10th, the Captain's birthday, which the men took as Providence. A little later, we saw with inexpressible joy the North Star above the horizon. In the night of February 21st, on the tribord side, I recognised the Isle of Fire of cap Vert, and proposed to Mr Neiret that he break out the ration of eau-de-vie. To set an example, Mr Neiret himself worked the pump for one hour of each watch, and I followed him.

West of the Açores, one of the sailors called sail, which the bo'sun recognised as the company ship, the *Chameau*, carrying wine from Bordeaux to Saint-Domingue. We put up the white ensign, and gave chase until she heaved-to. I bought two barrels of clairet, paid with a bill on the Company's agent at Cap-Français. It seemed I was doomed for ever to be the Company's debtor.

Once we had doubled the île aux Fleurs, the western-most of the isles of the Açores, the men were much relieved

and, though it was yet four hundred leagues to the har-
bours of France, felt themselves to be in home waters.
On March 10th, at eleven of the morning, a man called
sail astern, and for three days the vessel followed in our
furrow, always a league distant. On the fourth day, she put
up sail and closed to half a league. We could make out
three banks of guns.

"M. Neiret, would you be so kind as to give me the
use of your glass?"

I peered into the glare and then lowered the glass. In
as easy a tone as I could muster, I said: "The vessel is His
Britannic Majesty's First-Rate Ship-of-the-Line *Galatea*,
mounting seventy-two guns, Captain Baker commanding.
I saw her in Calcutta rode not ten months ago."

One of the petty officers swore.

I turned to Mr Neiret.

"Do I have your permission to descend to the gun-deck
and speak to your master-gunner?"

The master-gunner was named Lefebvre.

"Are you able, M. Lefebvre, to take your two heaviest
pieces into the Sainte-Barbe in the stern?"

He pointed to the timbers above his head, where iron
rings were bolted to the under-deck. He said: "Round shot
or mitraille?"

"We need to take down Mr Baker's masts."

Mr Lefebvre nodded. "Will you lift off *Atalante*'s stern, Colonel? Or shall I?"

"Leave it to me, sir." And then, from the ladder: "Who is Saint Barbara?"

"She protects cannoners and all who must work with artillery."

"Shall you call on her, M. Lefebvre?"

"I do not need to. She is with me."

On top, I said: "Gentlemen, within the space of one hour, we need to cut off the stern of this vessel. Mr Neiret needs every man, able-bodied or not, to man the saws."

"And where, Mr Landsman, shall we find another rudder?"

I had forgotten the rudder.

"Mr Baker shall provide it."

XLIV

Still *Galatea* beat on, always at a distance, like a tiger stalking an injur'd water-deer. Upwind of us, she could stop us dead whenever she wished. From her fore-gaillard, I saw a puff of smoke.

Mr Neiret sprang back, found his footing, then put his hand to his face.

"M. Neiret is hit!"

"Leave me. Leave me. It is spent."

From about two cable-distances, we heard a *porte-voiz* but could not make out a word.

"Is he speaking in English?"

"The hailer, if you please, Mr Bo'sun. WILL YOU SPEAK IN ENGLISH, CAPTAIN?"

The second speech was clear as burn-water.

"M. Neiret. Captain Baker orders you to lower your ensign and top sails, clew up your mainsels, heave to and come in your launch aboard *Galatea*. If you fire so much as a musket-shot, there shall be no quarter."

"What is the English for *rejeté*, Colonel?"

"Are we sawn through?"

"Sawn through, Colonel."

Two cables as thick as a man's wrist and tight as a whip held the transom.

"M. Lefebvre is ready?"

"He is ready, Colonel."

I raised the *porte-voix*. The white ensign slapped at my face.

"REFUSED."

Galatea came on. I could see lights running the length

of her gun-decks which filled me with dread.

"M. Neiret, is M. Baker within cannon-shot?"

"He is eating our wind. We are slowing."

"Two hundred yards."

I looked about me. Every man on the dunette was standing bolt-upright. Behind me, the sailors were armed to the teeth.

"One hundred and fifty yards."

"Draw sword, if you please, M. Neiret."

"Seventy-five yards."

We could see the English men, crowded on the fore-gaillard, without a care in the world.

"Now, sir."

I brought my sword down. With a grunt, the stern began to slip, and fall, and, at that same instant, a gust of heat rose up through the plankes. Even as the sound of shot reached us, there was a second blast of heat, as if some devil were working a pair of bellows, and then a third. We were engulfed in smoke. Through smoke and tears, I saw that *Galatea* was but a broken thing. Her masts hung at crazy angles and her decks were a foam of undulous white, like the morning bed of affectionate lovers. Mr Lefebvre had shot down the main mast, which had brought down the mizaine. The artimon was standing but had lost its lower spar, and her sails were torn to rags.

For one or more of the shots, Mr Lefebvre must have loaded canister. The fight had lasted one minute.

Without her canves, *Galatea* was slowing. Her bow-sprit was splintered, but beneath it her figure-head, bare-breasted, hair streaming, glided towards us like some emblem of fatal delight.

"The Captain!"

"M. Lefebvre! Shoot off the prow figure."

"He has not the elevation."

"Use small arms! Anything!"

The vessels bumped. *Atalante* shivered and groaned, but without anger or resentment, like an old ass under a pesant's wand.

I raised my sword. "See to the Captain! Boarding party! Advance!"

I swung onto *Galatea*'s bow-sprit. Glancing round, I saw my boarding party consisted of young Neiret.

"What are you doing, M. Neiret? How dare you leave your command! Return, at once."

Galatea's fore-gaillard was covered in splintered wood, cordage and snapping canvas. If there were any man above deck, he was buried under sail. Having to start somewhere, I took my knife and began cutting about a promising shape. I carved out a hat and then a red face. It blinked and winked and lurked. It was Mr Baker.

"Captain Béranger has given Lieutenant Neiret and your servant plenipotentiary powers to set terms. If you—"

"Don't I know you, sir?"

"Yes, Perrin's at Calcutta."

"Rather a nice place. I fancy I shall go again. Do they entertain ladies there?"

It is a twitch of some Englishmen, that I have long admired, always to seem to be thinking of something other than the matter before them.

With a couple more incisions, I had my patient standing. All about, English men were emerging like dusty insects from coucouns. I had been reinforced by two sailors, white as armed ghosts, pistols bobbing in their palsied hands.

"Mr Baker, I would have you stand down your gunners."

Captain Baker leered. "You stand them down. You said you were in command."

I tripped and hirpled back to the bow-sprit. I shouted: "I have only the top-deck. The gunners are stood-to. If they come broad-side of us, they will send *Atalante* to the bottom."

The maître said: "Baker will jump us. He has done it before. I say we cut 'em adrift."

There was general agreement.

Mr Neiret spoke. "Gentlemen! We need Mr Baker. In the event that we must abandon ship."

As one, we gaped at the lad. He blushed. I saw that Mr Neiret, a mere boy and alone of us, had been able to think the unthinkable: that, as the last resort, and to save his company, he would give the order to abandon *Atalante*. Even to me, who had the least connection with *Atalante*, the thought was treacherous, ungallant and unnatural. Yet in the way of such things, the thought had but to be put in words to become self-evident.

I shouted from *Galatea*: "Give me ten minutes. M. Neiret, would you kindly lend me for that time your pocket-watch?"

"But," Mr Neiret stuttered, "it was my father's."

"Weel, I shall do without."

The maître had in his hand the sand-glass used for the log. He turned it over.

I made my way over the canvas, where, from groans and oaths beneath me, I understood I was walking on living creatures. I cut my way to the main hatch, and began to descend. There was no light below but the matches of the guns. I saw a wall of faces and then a muzzle-flash. I skeltered up in a hail of missiles.

On deck, I had an inspiration. I ascended to the dunette, cut the halyarde of the Union flag, and wrapped myself in it. Thus protected by both Saint Andrew and Saint George, I stepped, stooping, onto the gun-deck.

I said in English: "Gentlemen! Do not kill me until you have heard what I have to say."

Every man had his knife or spike. The mousses, still with the cartridge-bags about their necks, darted forward, lunging with splinters of wood. Before me a man, his broad chest bare and piqued, whom I took to be the master-gunner, had his piece levelled at my chest.

"Mr Baker has struck his colours."

"Bugger Baker. And bugger you, fucking Jack shite."

I let the Jacobite affair go by.

I said: "In precisely two minutes of the glass, Second-Captain Neiret will cut *Galatea* and all of us adrift. You will have the pleasure of killing me in any way you deem just. A little later, you will be driven onto a lee-shore, or be carried into the ocean, where you will suck the canvas for water and feel one another's legs for fat and lean."

"Better than starving in a Frencher gaol."

"I promise you, gentlemen, that you shall not be prisoners-of-war but will be permitted to leave for England just as soon as H.M.S *Galatea* has been repaired and is in a condition to sail."

"Why should I trust you, Jackow?"

"Because I have put my life in your hands."

What happened next I have turned and turned in my mind, but still cannot believe. The gunner bent and, with his right hand alone, pulled the cannon onto its blocks. Such a feat of strength I believe I shall never again witness. The astonish'd mousses lowered their sticks, the gunners their spikes. I clattered up on deck to find Mr Baker and his officers standing, dazed and spiteful among the flapping sail-cloth, while on the stern of *Atalante*, Mr Neiret, with his back to me and his sword drawn, held off a ring of our petty officers.

I made my way to the Captain's quarters. In a furnace of sunlight, Mr Béranger lay beneath the breasts of *Galatea's* prow-figure, sleeping like an infant.

"Captain Béranger, Mr Baker is a-board and waits upon your terms."

There was a roar from the bed. Through the linen, Captain Béranger burst like a whale-fish. There was a crack as bone head hit pine titty.

"You allowed that drunkard on my ship? You let Jeremiah Baker set foot on *Atalante*? God damn you for a land-loving cunt, William, I will have you court-martialled."

"You cannot fucking court-martial me, Béranger, because I am not in your fucking service and never want anything to do with it again. That boy and your gunners have won you a valuable prize, which will draw on you the graces of His Majesty and the Directors and allow you to draw a-beam of some top-heavy widow of Lorient, while all you did was pleasure yourself between decks. By God, Béranger, you will give M. Neiret a quarter of the prize-money . . ."

"That will leave just a quarter for my people."

". . . from your fucking share, you fucking miser, and you can fucking mention him and Master-Gunner Lefebvre in your fucking despatch."

"Will you kindly stop swearing, William?"

"Forgive me, Captain Béranger. I am unused to sea-fights. They are unlike anything in my experience."

"You would oblige me, Colonel Neilson, if you would remove Captain Baker from *Atalante*. Pitch him into the sea. And his men. And scuttle his tub of a warship."

I came onto the dunette to find Mr Neiret looking discomposed and Captain Baker giving orders, as if to the manner born.

"Why is Captain Baker carrying off M. Béranger's eau-de-vie?"

"He requires it for his wounded."

"There are no fu . . ."

I checked myself.

". . . wounded. Except yourself, young man."

"Wounded? Me?" The lad looked at me in rapture.

"You have a contusion of the cheek, close to the right

eye. If you refuse to go down to the surgeon, I shall carry you down myself, so help me."

The boy staggered below.

"Mr Baker, I am instructed to offer you the following terms. If you consent to return to your dismasted ship, and allow her to be hauled to Bayonne, Nantes or Lorient, you will be treated as if you are under furlough. New pine masts will be supplied and, during that time, you and your men will have free passage in the town and two leagues in all directions, excepting only the port enclose. Once H.M.S *Galatea* is sea-worthy, you will be permitted to leave with your men and arms and your colours at full-mast, and with all your gear except your cargo which belongs to H.V.C.M. and Mr Béranger. In addition, Captain Béranger will write to the Admiralty in London, giving account of how your fair conduct preserved your command."

Captain Baker looked untempted.

"In the meantime, I have been commanded to offer succour to your wounded. How much brandy do your surgeons require?"

"Six dozen? Eight dozen?"

"I shall see it carried over to your vessel." I turned and saw young Neiret, bandaged to the eye-balls. "M. Neiret, would you kindly ensure the terms of the convention are notarised and signed by both commanders? Also, can you spare a couple of invalids to place seals on the English vessel's cargo, lest it suffer shrinkage in the air of the Bay? And then, M. Neiret, you must bring these two ships into the Bay, and win us through to French water. How does that feel, young man? Who else of your friends has not one but two commands?"

"That shall not be necessary, Colonel Neilson."

I turned to see the ghastly figure of Captain Béranger, in night-shirt and -cap, in billows of tobacco smoke.

"I shall thank you not to intermeddle in marine affairs, Colonel Neilson, of which you know less than nothing."

I was in disgrace. I heard men say that it had been better *Atalante* had taken a broad side and gone down than the Captain's name put to so shameful a treaty. Barred from the after-decks, I was chased also from admidships, for the petty officers had hoped to plunder Baker's chests and his officers' cabins, held the spoil to be theirs and had already divided it between each *plat* or mess. I cruched in the spray at the bow, beside the commodities. I would have starved had not, in the night-watches, good Mr Neiret brought me treats from the Captain's table, such as a weevilly galette or a husk of salt beef. I slept with my sodden pistols in my lap. Beyond our stern, I could make out *Galatea*, wandering like a dottard on four cables. From her came not a sound, except, when the wind was full behind, snatches of song or shouts of rage or exultancy.

XLV

In the approaches to Lorient, Captain Béranger began in stages to dress himself. Passing through the reefs, I saw he had on shoes and stockings; at the île de Groix, he was wearing his cocked-hat; and, by the time, we came into Lorient road with the church bells a-ringing and flags on every lum and finial and cheering to the clouds, he was full-dressed excepting only his cravate. From *Galatea*, there was but somnolence.

I did not recognise Lorient. On the hill beside the wind-mills, a signal tower of stone commanded the whole firth. In place of the clutter and debriss of twenty years before, there were wharves and floating pontoons, an engine for erecting masts, a hall of merchandise with its peristyle, and three slipways with keels on the stocks, crowded by stacks of oak boards. The smoke from the forges blew into our faces. Everywhere was industry. We passed within a great chain or boom against English or Dutch attack and moored, side to side, against one of the pontoons. I had thought that, because I had not changed, the world had stayed as it was.

On the quay, there was a mob of people. As the officers and men descended, musketeers with bayonets fixed held the people back lest painted cloths and other pacotilles pass from ship to shore without the Company's say-so.

Only Mr Lefebvre bade me farewell. He was in high good humour.

"On a long campaign, Mr Neilson, such brouleries happen. I have seen ships bump and lumber into port, with the officers blazing away all-against-all on the dunette, and sailors lying gutted in the bilges. You will be friends once more on land." He tipped his hat, and bounded down the companionway to the pontoon.

I rose and touched the rail. I said out loud: "Good-bye, sweet *Atalante*. Long may you stay tied-up at this dock, while cadets learn their ropes upon your decks and swing from your rigging till you sink into the mud and turn, as we all must, into our constituent atoms."

Yet I stayed to survey the scene. My eyes were drawn to a neat lady in black, pretty as a picture, soaking Lieutenant Neiret in tears and kisses. The lad submitted in discomfort, compounded by two little girls swinging on his thighs. At a distance of some ten or twelve feet, Mr Béranger stood, in a clean uniform and brushed wig, his hat clamped under his arm, and on his face a look of marine benevolence.

Mr Neiret disentangled himself. "Sir, may I present my mother, Mme Neiret?"

"Gentleman to lady, M. Neiret. Always gentleman to lady."

"Maman, may I introduce Captain Béranger, as kind and brave and good a captain as any lad could wish?"

"I am honoured to meet my son's captain, sir."

"I do not wish to interrupt your reunion, and shall not detain you, Mme Neiret, but I feared that I might not have another opportunity to speak to you. I wished only to say this: Your son's deportment on the campaign, madame, was never less than good and on one occasion it was exemplary. May I take my leave?"

"Will you not honour my Jérôme, I mean M. Neiret, with a visit, sir?"

"I near forgot, madame. Heigh-ho, you scamps, which of you is to have the fruit of Portugal?"

He held out an orange.

The little girls looked at the brilliant fruit and then at each other. They were inseparable. Neither could take what the other could not also have. Their eyes began to mist. Béranger tossed the orange in the air and two came down, which he caught in each hand and without dropping his hat. (Every child in India can do that trick.)

"By magic! The orange becomes a pair!"

The girls seized the treasures and retired to a heap of coiled rope.

"You are kind, Captain Béranger," Mme Neiret said.

"I am much in business, madame, so I shall be brief. I have a design to give your son a fifth of my share of the prize-money. My interest can do a little for him, but it never harmed a young officer to have some property, and the scamps one day will need ..."

He turned a melting eye on the girls who were eating the oranges as if those were all the dowry they would require.

"Unfortunately, madame, while to you Ensign-Lieutenant Neiret is a strong hand and support, he is by the laws of France a minor. He shall require your power-of-attorney."

The lady looked terrified. Poor Neiret seemed to tack between pride and black hatred.

"Do not fear, madame. I refuse absolutely to give this task to one of my officers or expose you to the ogles of clerks and lackeys at the hôtel of the Company of the Indies. This day, in one week, you will be kind enough to send your officer – my officer! – to dig me out of the magazines. I shall endeavour to use no more than a quarter-hour of your time."

"Sir, we are not well-to-do, but you will greatly honour

our house." She dropped the bonniest curtesie you ever saw.

"Now please, dear Mme Neiret, you absolutely must dismiss me. I am on His Majesty's business."

Captain Béranger walked away, but a sort of languor fell on him, as if the interview had cost him more than he had designed.

I turned in disgust, then pulled myself together. A sailor a-courting is a horrid sight to see. For myself, I would call on my old hostess and we would laugh at our grey hairs. I waited until the crowd had dispersed.

The clartie old bourg beyond the rope walk had been razed. In its place was a desert of straight streets. The muddy lane where once I used to wander to the Ploemeur bridge and water-mill was closed by bastions laid out by military engineers. Bewildered, and quite unused to walking, I inquired from jostling foot passengers the way to the house of Mme Julie. They marked me for a rustic or foreigner, waved at the market place and hurried on. When I stood out to allow ladies to pass, they smiled and seemed to say to themselves: At least, some gentlemen remember the old ways! It was as if I had been in a place where the hours passed at a lesser velocity.

Mme Julie's establishment was now an inn, with a rattling sign-board, the Duc de Rohan. In the stable-yard, a big man was belling orders. I did not wish to cause my friend embarrassment, and took a whole bed at the Golden Lion at the other side of the place. I was in a humour, for it is in the nature of the man that what he does not want to have for himself, he does not want another to have. I wrote to Mme Julie, announcing that I was at Lorient, but the scullion came back without a reply. Women are free to give preference, as poor Jérôme Neiret would soon find out. I would say that women understand better than men such things.

In my chamber, which looked upon the church and market, I felt more tossed about than on the sea off the Cape. Even in the Castle of the Bastille, or in the gaol of *Atalante* back in '27, I had not felt so cast down. Here I was, returned to Europe, forty years of age, and without a friend or a penny to my name.

I had fought my country and made myself a stranger to my family and for what: absolute government and Champagne wine? For those advantages, must I crak with Ugolino and the traitors in the frozen lake? Had I friends or family to regard or judge me, I would be a ridiculous thing.

In time, the window darkened and with it my thoughts. Futile battles jangled in my head. The friends I had – Joanic Tareau, poor François, Father O'Crean – had fallen into the deep. Why has Providence preserved me, when better men have fallen down?

I sought to conjure the île de France, and the time I

served Mme de Maurepas as equerie, but something like a barrier or a wall stood in my way. I saw the island only as I had seen it half a year past in its prosperity. I saw the African women and girls in their gay clothes in the porch of Father Borthon's church. When I tried to pass them, and to enter whatever was beyond them, I could find no shape nor colour nor scent, only darkness.

In despair, I summoned that night at the Royal Bank at Paris, and sought her figure among the scaffalds, but nothing would stay in place. Walls, windows, scaffalds, soffits leaned and tumbled down in a cloud of plaster-dust. I sought her smile, but it had vanished with Mr Law and the bank-notes and the Duke-Regent into oblivion.

Twenty-five years had passed since I had seen her for the first time and, since the last time, near eighteen years. Had she truly smiled at me through the scaffalds? Was it she who sent me priceless books in prison? Had she worn at Port-Louis a dress of Masulipatnam cloth and spectacles tied with a ribbon? Had she truly said: "What are you doing, Mr Neilson?" Were those true impressions or mere fancies that I had conjured out of dreams to keep my courage up? I had thought I would ever hold her image in my heart and all my thoughts and all my actions would be known to her. I saw at last that I had no recollection of her, nor she of me, for how could she or any person, man or woman, be more faithful than I had been. The contraption of my life had been kicked away, and I came tumbling down.

The pain was unendurable. I sprang up, paced the room, plunged outside but the dark streets were encumbered with the sodden bodies of sailors from the two vessels just tied up. From the alleys came cries of pleasure or encouragement from the gallant women drawn out of Nantes and Rennes by the prise. I thought that I, too, must drink, to dull the pain in my heart, and returned to the Golden Lion, but Captain Baker was roaring over a table of twenty men and forty bottles, at Mr Béranger's expense. I skulk'd into the common part, where sailors sat alone amid tangles of smoke. My host brought a bottle of brandy and a glass, and I asked him to leave them with me. The pain began to dull. I thought: A couple more of these bottles and I'll be linking arms with Baker, and matching him toast for toast.

As the pain abated, so my mind began to open. A thought came in and took possession of the place. I saw that it was not the marine element of the fight that had unmanned me, and caused me to insult Mr Béranger, but the fight itself. I was losing my nerve which was, by some connexion that I could not fathom, bound to my love for Mme de Maurepas. I saw that my profession was no more. I was a danger, not so much to myself, for I did not care about myself, but to men of my command. It was time to end my life before I did good men an injury.

I would finish my bottle, and another, then go next-doors and pistol Mr Baker, whom I did not like, and in the medley die in dishonour or, should I survive the fight, swing from *Atalante*'s fore-yard-arm.

Such a plan, so sage in conception and simple in execution, I did not put in practice. There are words that will stop an army, and a single word stopped me. That word was ÉCOSSE, which is the French for Scotland. Two gentlemen, one pale from town and the other sun-burnt from the sea, had fled Mr Baker's racket and were speaking in my ear-shot. I heard that His Christian Majesty had shipped an army of Jacks to Scotland, commanded by King James' son, now proclaimed Prince of Wales. They had gathered the Highland clans and some of the lowland gentlemen, taken all Edinburgh but the castle, and shatter'd a royal army under Mr Cope by the bleachings at Tranent. King James was even now hovering off the coast of Scotland.

Here was my Providence. I would tie the ends of my life in the place where it had begun. In one swoop, I would discharge my duty to brave Father O'Crean, kneel at my mother's grave and assist, if they would accept assistance from a renegade, my brethren and sisters. If matters went ill for me, I would sleep for all time under the heather.

PART 8

Scotland, 1746

XLVI

At the Company's hôtel, a plump packet awaited me,
pompous with seals. In it, His Majesty ordered me to
Dunkerque to guard a shipment of five hundred muskets,
twenty thousands of powder and eight cases of ball to be
delivered at Montrose or any other harbour or anchorage
in Scotland under the controle of France or her allies. I
was to place myself under the orders of Captain Douvry,
privateer of that town, engaged in the King's service.

In the diligence, I felt as strange as ever I did. Where
my heart had been was a sort of elation, without trace of
the self or even of humanity, like the wind I remember as
a boy on the top of Trahenna Hill. I was going to rest
and in the loveliest land on earth and the heath would
bloom and fade above me for eternity.

It was night when the chaise reached Dunkerque. *La*

Marie, lately detached from its commerce into the King's service, was out in the water. Her boat awaited me at the head of a long jetée beyond the sea-side fortifications. A cold wind blew into my bones. A shape appeared before us, which hardened into a long and svelte yacht, riding low in the water. I had hoped to have made an inventorie of the munitions, but it was too late for all that. Sails were going up about me and I heard the grinding of the anchor cabestan. I had no choice but to trust in Mr Douvry.

Who did not recommend himself. By the lantern attached to the main mast, I could make out the wheel and a man before it, without coat or shoes, but with a red bonnet and an air of independency.

"Captain Douvry?"

"Haste-ye, Mr Neilson. We have waited for ye time enough."

I found a space for myself and wrapped my cloack about me. The sailors, who appeared to be about a half-dozen in number, as they moved about their manoevre, trod on my feet and elbowed me. As for Mr Douvry, his eyes flickered every few moments to the top-mast where an item of cloth, which looked once to have belonged in some lady's inner garment, flutter'd with the breeze. From the cold that knifed me, and the white water under the bow, I sensed that we were racing.

"Light ahead. Ten degrees to tribord."

My landsman's eyes could make out nothing.

"Take station, friends. Now, not a sound from you, Mr Neilson."

I could still make out nothing in the murk. Then all became light as if from a hundred suns. Before us, a warship reared like a cliff, drenched in light. I could make out the ripples in her canvas, and the twist of her cables and rigging. Above us, a fusee was dipping towards our deck.

"Have a care of the powder, Mr Neilson."

I drenched my cloack in the bilges and had it ready to quell a spark. From the warships on each side, rockets were fizzeling upwards and bursting in air.

From the gun-deck of the vessel not twenty yards on our beam, I could hear shouted orders. There was a wave of heat. It seemed we passed each gun-port only a second before it vomited heat.

We came alongsides the quarter-deck, bathed in the rocket-light. One of the English officers must have looked at Mr Douvry in a strange way or in some other fashion displeased him. Mr Douvry took his right hand off the wheel, drew his pistol from his belt, shot the man in the face, passed me the hot pistol to recharge, and returned his right hand to the wheel.

We were not pursued.

For some time, I could neither see from the flashes or hear from the cannon. After an hour or two, the maître lit the lantern. I took that as a signal that I might speak.

"May I ask you, Mr Douvry, how much His Majesty pays you for these jaunts?"

"Ye may ask, but I shan't tell ye."

We fell into silence.

"One hundred thousand francs, if ye must know. But it is ..."

He searched for a word he might have heard but once.

"Imaginary, Mr Douvry?"

"Yes, imaginary."

"You might petition in place of the cash an honour, such as a barony or viscounty. Those cost His Majesty nothing and are more readily conferred."

"What would I want with a baronay or viscountay?"

"You might not want the honour, but your daughters ..."

"I have seven daughters. Or is it twelve? I cannot provide for all of them."

We slid back into silence.

Something I had said interested Mr Douvry, for some time later he turned to me and, with his head in parallel with the deck, said:

"What duties are required of a viscount, Colonel Neilson?"

"None whatsoever. You continue doing what you are doing now, M. Douvry. You need make no alteration in your furrow of life."

"I love this life. Don't ye, M. Neilson?"

"Not so much as I was used to."

XLVII

The day passed in rain. We could see but a cable's length ahead, which was all to the good. We dined in a high style, with fish and salads and wine enough to assuage the hardiest tippler. I inquired from Mr Douvry the bill-of-lading, which he recited from memory, with bad grace. It seemed to me that, for Mr Douvry, these wars of kings and nations were not of themselves of especial moment, but were necessary variabilities alike the wind, the tide, the weather and the rate of exchange.

By dawn of the third day, we were off the coast of Scotland.

"Shall we put in at Mont-Rose, Mr Neilson?"

I searched the dock with my glass, from left to right and back again. There was nobody to be seen in the falling rain.

"No, sir."

"And why not, M. Neilson?"

"The French standard is upside-down."

Mr Douvry put up his glass and nodded. The vessel swung into the wind. "We shall try Angernesse."

"You shall need a pilot for the estuary, Captain Douvry."

"A pilot, you say, M. Neilson. My friends, the Colonel says that we shall need a pilot for the Morey."

There was a cannibal laugh.

"I did not intend in any way to belittle your . . ."

"Well, then, shall we hear less of your pilots?"

We fell into sulks, interrupted, every now and then, by that phantom and never-again-to-be-spoken word. I had not known, up to then, that pirates were so susceptible and apt to take offence. Off the town of Nairn, I saw shipping close in, and on the far bank of the Nairn river what appeared to be an extensive camp. When I asked Mr Douvry to take us as close as he thought prudent for the safety of his command, so that I might estimate the enemy strength, he hissed, made as if to pronounce the forbidden vocable of P, and tacked to the opposite shore.

As we passed up the Frith against the flood, Mr Douvry ditty-dathered. *Marie* all but struck in the Narrows then drifted onto the Black Isle side where the ebb was at its strongest. Canvas rattled across the deck. The boom swung like a tavern door in a rout. The play was lost on me.

I looked in delight at the soft hills, flooded with cloud, smelled heath and peat smoke, and inhaled the purity of Scotland. Finding me a spoil-sport, Mr Douvry took in sail and glided into the Ness river. We tied up at the so-called New Harbour beneath the Citadel, which somebody had seen fit lately to demolish.

I was seeing to the munitions, when Mr Douvry took his leave.

He said: "I shall come back for ye, M. Neilson."

"I cannot pay your tariff, Captain Douvry."

"No generous friend, or loving mistress?"

"Alas! Nothing like that, Captain Douvry."

"Pity," he said and walked away.

A little later, an officer brought me a note from Lord George Murray, the army commander, saying that Mr McCarrick had fallen sick of the pleurisy and I was to command his troop of foot. I was bidden to a council of war at Culloden House some three or four miles to the south-east of town, where I should be presented to the Prince of Wales.

"Has His Majesty landed?"

"No, sir. The Prince of Wales commands."

A Highland man brought me a poney and led me the way.

XLVIII

Culloden House was a fine stone place, the seat of Mr Forbes, President of the Session, who had taken himself to the isles. I was shown into the dining-room, where general officers formed a ring at a lighted table, while other men lounged against the walls. Fires spat and smoked on two hearths but conveyed to my Indian flesh not a crum of heat. I was announced to Lord George, who looked up but said nothing. Lord Elcho led me down and up and presented me to the other officers. The last was a gentleman in French military uniform, whom I recognised.

I said: "Sir, you agreed to a meeting which I was prevented from attending. I am ready now to wait on you."

Lord George looked up from the table. "For God's sake, gentlemen, will you not have fighting and to spare tomorrow?"

The Chevalier Durfort bowed to him. "Some years ago, sir, in the Indies, I did this officer an injury. It would shame me to fall tomorrow without having given him satisfaction."

I turned to Mr Durfort. "Let us shake hands, Joseph. It would please our mistress."

Lord George lost his temper. "Will the French officers leave off just for an instant of an instant from their blessed mistresses! Attention, gentlemen!"

He stood and fell into a bow. Above the bent backs, I saw the famous Prince of Wales. He was in the prime of youth, tall and well-made, and of a fair complexion. He wore a tartan short coat and blue bonnet. On his breast was the green ribbon and star of the Order of Saint Andrew or, as we call it, the Thistle. Beneath a light-coloured pereuyk, his face showed weariness or indifference.

"Sire, may I present Colonel Neilson, of the French service, lately arrived with supply at Inverness. He is to command McCarrick's."

"I think a countryman of ours, Lord George?"

"I was born in the Cowgate of Edinburgh, sire, and hope soon to have the honour of showing Your Royal Highness its overlooked beauties."

Prince Charles Edward Stuart smiled and touched my shoulder. "I am glad to have you with me, Colonel Neilson."

After a time, the Prince and his train left the room. The council diddled awhile and broke up. Lord George called me over.

"Forgive me my humour, Colonel Neilson. We are right pleased to see you and have your supply."

"Are the men in good spirit, Lord George?"

"It is not the men that occupy me, Mr Neilson. They stood like devils at Falkirk. It is His Royal Highness. His heart is no longer in the fight."

"A good display tomorrow will restore it."

Lord George looked at me and, then, after making some adjustments for my black skin and India calico-coat, smiled as to himself.

McCarrick's were camped about a mile to the south at the place called Drummossie Moor. It was not a military position, but I thought it best not to agitate the men so late in the day. There would be time enough before battle. A weary officer with a dirty wig, Lieutenant O'Malley, brought me the strength, such as it was. One hundred and ninety-two men, two lieutenants (himself and Mr Sizar) and two sergeants. No captain, surgeon, chaplain or pay-master. One piper and two drummer-lads.

A fire was burning. I sat down on a stack of pine by the fire and lit my pipe. After a while, I said:

"Come to me, men."

They gathered in the firelight. I knocked out my pipe and stood up. I said: "I am Neilson, and I have been in fights that would cause your bonnie hair to stand on end. If tomorrow you do precisely as I command, we shall do very well. Our cause is just, our strength equal to the enemy or better, and we have beaten him at every fight since His Royal Highness came here.

"For victory, you do not need me. Mr O'Malley and Mr Sizar can win you battles. But I have known defeat and defeat asks more of a man than victory. Yesterday is obliterated, and there shall be no tomorrow, and the whole of time comes down to a single moment. In that moment there is only you and your brothers-in-arms, and your captain, and our Blessed Lady standing at his shoulder. Then you shall watch my every movement, and jump to my every word, and with Her Blessed help, I shall bring you out of the wreck.

"Yet I have seen, in certain places and times, something beyond defeat, and beyond death and life. When I have fallen, and Lieutenant O'Malley, and Sergeant Doyle and Danny and Conor, and Little Arthur, when Our Lady turns away Her face in tears and God Himself sickens, yet you will stand, my good and brave soldiers, and show what men were in our times. And three hundred years from now, when all other things of our age have been forgotten, when the heather comes to flower and the meadow-pipits sing and a hen-buzzard mews in the high air, strange people will say: Here, on the day of battle, in the wreck of the world, Neilson's Irish men stood and fought till they could stand and fight no more."

From the darkness, there was a clap of hands.

"Very nice," someone drawled in English. "Eloquent."

The vicomte Durfort stepped into the fire-light. With him were four orderlies, carrying paniers of Champagne.

He said: "Irish soldiers, one of the merits of His Very Christian Majesty's officers is their unstinting care for supply."

From the men, there was not a sound.

"Thank the gentleman, men."

There was a roaring and cheering.

"Give the men a drink, Mr O'Malley, and take one yourself. Then be so kind as to bring us a cup. This officer wishes to speak to me apart."

Once we were settled in the heather, Mr Durfort said: "What is a hen-buzzard?"

"Have you come to tease me, Joseph?"

"Wait."

O'Malley poured out the Champagne for us. While Mr Durfort had with him a blazoned silver cup, I had half a shell casing.

"Have the men to lie down, Mr O'Malley. Have they drink for tomorrow?"

"There is potine."

O'Malley walked away towards the fire.

"I fancy the sound of potine."

"It is the Irish Armagnac. Finer, some say."

"I rather think I shall take a dash of your potine, tomorrow."

He looked up at the sky.

"What is on your mind, Joseph?"

"She has retired to France, to a nasty little property in the Sologne, all battlements and blazons, sees nobody but her confessor, counts her money. Half the busted gallants of the district parade before her gates, but she won't let 'em in."

"Why are you telling me this, Joseph?"

"I am telling you this, William, because it is time. It is possible, though not especially likely, that I, as His Royal Highness's aide-de-camp, will get off the field tomorrow. You, William, shall not nor any of your men. I do not know if she loved you in the île de France and, even if she did, she would not love you now."

A specimen of the Caledonian ornithologia flapped and glided above us, but I dispersed her with a glare.

"What I can say with certainty is that Mme la marquise de Maurepas never loved me."

We leaned back and looked up at the sky.

He said: "Please don't take this amiss, William, but I cannot now remember the nature of the injury I did you."

"Nor can I. Wait! You told Mme la marquise of my challenge."

"I most certainly did not, William. How could you think that of me?"

"I admit it sounds unlikely."

After a while, I said:

"Let His Royal Highness go, Joseph, if he wishes. I would not want him paraded at the Tolbooth of Edinburgh and his head in a fishwife's basket."

"Rather my own feeling, dear friend." He rolled himself into his cloak. Rain was falling, and then snow. He said: "I find, William, that the amenities of your homeland have been overdrawn." Then he fell asleep.

XLIX

I woke to find Mr Durfort departed, the fires cold and the men unoccupied.

"Have the men breakfasted?"

"They will not eat before battle, sir."

"What did you say, Mr O'Malley?"

"I mean, sir . . ."

"By God, the men shall eat breakfast even if I have to broil their pease-and-bacon myself and stand over them while they take it."

"Yes, sir."

After the men had breakfasted, I had O'Malley move them to a new station some eighty yards up a small slope.

It was a cosie position, with a morass in front and a stone sheep enclosure to the right, and beyond that the Water of Nairn. The slight elevation allowed me to see our force, in a single line stretching as far as the policies of Culloden House, the Highland men each by clan or nation under their usual commander, with among them the blue of our French regular soldiers. Because of our depleted strength, my force was placed in reserve along with two other battalions to our left.

Rain was falling, which turned at times to blirts of snow and hail. To occupy the men, and keep them from stiffening or thinking overly, I set them to dismantling a portion of the wall and carrying the stones to make a narrow causey through the marsh, which I had marked at each end by a private arrangement of the stones.

"Mr O'Malley, what is the efficient range of the men's firelocks?"

"I don't . . . I shall find out, Colonel Neilson."

"Very good, Mr O'Malley. When you have found out, will you have a man plant a marker at that point on the causey?"

Prompt at noon, three English columns came into sight to the north-east, and formed a triple line each of five battalions. It seemed to me that the formation was rather

one of defence than assault, for placed between each battalion were three cannon and their gunners, the void in the
rank covered by the battalion in the line behind. Before
our position, on the far left of the English army and about
five hundred yards distant, were two or more squadrons
of dragoons. I imagined that they had orders to attempt to
outflank our right wing and get in behind the Highland
men.

Joseph was everywhere. As he gallopped between the
armies, I heard single shots ripping from the enemy like
a lady's dress tearing on floor clouts. Seeing me, he reined
in and stopped dead.

"The Highland men have been marching all night.
Lord George and the Prince had an idea to make a night
attack."

"So, why did Lord George and His Royal Highness
not make a night attack?"

"They lost themselves in your unforgiving country."

"Well, no harm done. I have sent to Lord George to
inform him of my change of position."

He looked at my toiling men. "William, what are you
doing?"

Joseph looked again. "Oh!" he said. "Very strategical."

He stood up in his stirrup-irons and shouted: "Irish
men! Yesterday I brought you Champagne. Yet today,

when I had hoped to bathe my throat in the elixir of Finne and Coucullane, what do I receive?"

Sergeant Burke ran up with a metal beaker. Joseph drank its contents in one swallow.

"Excellent," he said. "With such a fire in your entrails, no army on earth will resist you." As he gave spur, he softly said to me: "The Prince is in better heart. I wonder if we may not prevail over these Germans."

As he galloped away, the English guns started up.

The essence of a pitched battle is not to commit first, for that must ever open breaches in the line. Men are held up by obstacles and bad ground, or broken by fire, or lose their officers or their nerve. The pounding had barely begun when it became too much. There was a whooping and a yelling, and the ground shook under feet. Our line was advancing at the run. My position was not especially elevated, and anyway smoke and mist limited my vision, but I sensed our left was held or falling, because our right was turning in. I thanked the Providence that had caused me to move station. I could see the enemy dragoons stamping, but they could not turn our right without being enfiladed by my men. They might dismantle the enclosure walls to outflank us, but cavalrymen are generally too fine for that sort of work, and my people would make it warm enough for them. If they wished to have some part in the fight, they must first drive us off and, since we would not go, they would have to kill us.

Through the smoke, Highland men were streaming towards us, heads bowed, plaids flapping in the wind. Lieutenant O'Malley drew sword and took a pace forward.

"Stand, you dogs!"

"Do not rally them, sir! Open to double interval! If they have broken once, they will break again."

"Their powder, m'sieur!"

"They shall need it more than you shall."

The clan men passed like ghosts between the files. I did not think the battle would take up much of our time.

All over the field, I sensed rather than saw that our men were falling back: some in a semblance of order, some ragged but still under orders, and others in individual flight. The enemy gunners were loading canister, which whistled and shrieked about us. Then, by one of those quirks that occur on the battlefield, the smoke and mist rolled away, the sun broke through, and I saw, but a gunshot away, the Prince of Wales in a knot of officers.

The prince was beside himself. He had drawn his sword, and appeared to be calling for a second assault. His people, among whom I recognised his old governor, Mr Sheridan, were urging him to mount. Beyond, a party of enemy cavalrymen were riding at him full-tilt.

Something flashed at my right. It was Joseph, at top gallop, upright in his irons. He stood up on the saddell, and jumped to ground, while his mount collided with the leading enemy. He rose to his feet, lifted the Prince of Wales onto his horse, and with the flat of his sword struck the animal on the rump. The animal plunged forward, the Prince rattling and bumping like a string-puppet. Then Colonel the vicomte Durfort turned about and stood, in the way that he had, lounging upright, until the red tide engulfed him.

By coincidence, Mme de Maurepas will lose her equirries within minutes the one of the other. With luck, she shall not hear of it. Before me, the dragoons must have been thinking: Why don't he run away, like everybody else?

The men were looking queasie.

"Sergeants, break out the ration."

The sounds of battle had fallen away. We were the last men standing on the French side. I heard the clatter of teeth on tin. Without turning, I said: "Take your drink, men, and while you do so, mind that, whatever happens in the next five minutes, you are soldiers of France."

"You may be, monsieur, but we are Irish men and we have lost our relish for your fight."

"*Fir na hÉireann!* Men of Ireland! Did you think I would leave you? Did you think I would suffer these

Saxons to touch a hair of your fine red heads? *Ó Máille!*
We shall now perform a little wee manoeuvre. If you listen,
and do entirely as I command, we shall do very well.

"At the bottom of the slope before you, you will see
some Saxon cavalrymen who appear to bear a resentment
towards us. You'll mind, no doubt, a young fellow curvet-
ting on a bay horse. That is Captain Chumley, who has the
small estate of Tugby in the English county of Leicester-
shire. He is, as you can see, a capital horseman and hopes
this day to gain immortal glory by killing us all. Except,
he cannot decide precisely when. Our task, my handsome
Irish men, is to hurry him along a pace.

"When I stop speaking, but not before, you are to break
silence and ranks. Throw down your packs, knock over the
colours, curse the Prince of Wales, abuse me to Hell, call
on our Blessed Mother, run this way and that, do what you
will. Give every sign that you are broken men, except that
you are not. While you are diddle-daddling, Mr Sizar ..."

"Yes, sir."

". . . take sixty men over the dyke and down behind
it, out of sight, loaded double charge. What charge,
Mr Sizar?"

"Double charge, sir."

"Now on our side of the dyke, Mr O'Malley!"

"Yes, sir."

"Mr O'Malley walks through the riot with his sword drawn. If you are on his sword side, you stay on that side. If you are on his finger-ring side, you stay on that side. When you see our friend give spur to his horse, you form two ranks of sixty men. When I give the order (and not before), you will aim and fire and go to ground, where you will fix bayonets and form square. And then, when Mr Chumley and his friends have gone away, we will promene down our wee causey through the mire and see if any of these foolish people dare to fight with us.

"Now! Go to! And try, if you can, not to shoot your officers."

You never saw such a medley. The standards were thrown down. O'Malley had his wig knocked off. Curses and cries rolled over the moor. I sought with my glass Mr Chumley, if that indeed was his name. On his face was a look that I misliked: as on the face of a man when his mistress consents. He gave spur to his horse. His troop, which was facing in every direction, spun like a carriage-wheel in mud.

Behind me, there was not a sound. I did not turn lest the men think I had not faith in them. Captain Chumley rode into a dip. As he crested the rise, he must have seen something, for he pulled hard, and his mount came up on her hind legs. It was too late. His troop, more or less in line, came over at full gallop. He spurred on, hoping for the best, and at once became bogged down.

"Lennán can take the officer, sir!"

"I can drop the little shite, monsieur."

"Leave him be, Mr Lennán."

Through a mist of black mud and spray, the lighter horses were winning through. I searched my marker in the ground.

"Now, dear friends. Front rank. Make ready. Look along your guns, and fire low.

"Front rank! Present!

"Front rank! Fire!

"Front rank! Down! Middle Rank! Present!

"Middle rank. Fire!

"Middle rank. Down on the ground!

"Dyke rank! Fire.

"All men to fix bayonet and rise!"

Before us was a curtain of smoke. It was as if we were at the theatre. Every now and then, a figure stumbled through on foot, reeking of blood and water, and fell; or a loose horse passed dragging its rider before turning back behind the curtain.

Little by little, the smoke lifted. The slaughter was not great. A couple of dozen men lay in every posture in the bog-cotton and rushes, and as many horses. One hundred and ninety-two musket balls, how well-aimed soever, are never going to do much hurt. For all that, the 10th Dragoons (Chumley's) had ceased to exist for that day, and perhaps for all days. Of Mr Chumley, there was no sign. On the dyke, a horse was spreadeagled, bellowing in pain. A pistol shot (Sizar's) silenced it. I turned. The men were staring at me.

"Unfix bayonets! Recharge muskets!"

Somebody broke the silence:

"It appears that monsieur has been to the wars afore."

There was a cheer.

"Silence in the ranks! You are the finest soldiers it has ever been my privilege to direct. Mr O'Malley! I will not waste these faithful men in a lost fight. Have them form column. Colours furled. No drum, no pipe. I am taking these men with me to France."

I stepped onto the causey. I had chosen to go forward, in part because the enemy would not expect that, and in part because I believ'd the river-crossing in our rear would be clogged with broken men and hag-ridden by enemy cavalry. In such a shambles, even the best soldiers may lose their discipline and formation. I had an idea that the English would let us go. They could stop us, but they would lose another troop of horse, and why would the Duke of Cumberland tarnish his great victory? Anyway, there were easier pickings from men not facing the front.

I intended to ford the river, for the Water of Nairn, though a noble stream, is no Ganges. I thought I would have no shortage of volunteers to stand with me on the near bank while the main body crossed. We would saunter up into Badenoch, the country of the MacPhersons, and come down one starless night to the isles and splash across to Mull, where Mr Douvry would be cruising for paying passengers in waters no English warship could draw in. I must see to victual, for we shall eat Mr MacPherson out of hoose and hame. Now were there some Whig laird hereabouts, with an overplus of fat cattle . . .

"William! For God's sake, look!"

Before me, at about one hundred and fifty yards distance, was a battery of guns. How did they bring them up in so short a time?

"Wheel left! Open ranks! At the double!"

As we charged, I could see artillery men falling all down the line. Is there nothing these Irish men cannot do? Behind the guns, on horseback, was a large young man with, across his chest, the blue ribbon of the Order of the Garter. Then all turned to smoke and heat, and my men were falling in a rain of fire and earth and black water.

We were closing.

I shouted: "Mr Lennán! Come to my side! At the double!"

From my left, a lad was running at me, head bowed, prancing over the fallen men like a deer. His face was black with powder and his long hair streamed behind him under his cap. I thought: If any boy deserves to live on this earth, it is this Lennán. Then where had been his head and flowing hair was nothing, his trunk spun in air and tumbled to the earth. Behind him, on our left, the smoke turned gold and red and all around were whistling blades, or as if a million stinging insects had turned in rage upon us. My coat hung on me in tatters and blood was streaming from my shirt and hands. With a last effort of thought, I saw that a hidden battery, at right angles to the first, was firing canister.

Something hit me in the belly and I fell down.

I pushed the dead man off.

"Is any man standing? Rally to me, lads."

The guns had ceased. I could hear nothing but whispers of pain and despair.

I thought: I have killed my Irish men. Not all eternity will wipe out my crime. I shall not need the flames of Hell for I have torments and a surplus to bring down with me.

I lifted myself to my feet, drew sword and walked towards the gentleman with the blue ribbon. I saw him incline his head and an officer running to the guns. I saw the gunners snap to it, and the matches flare and come down.

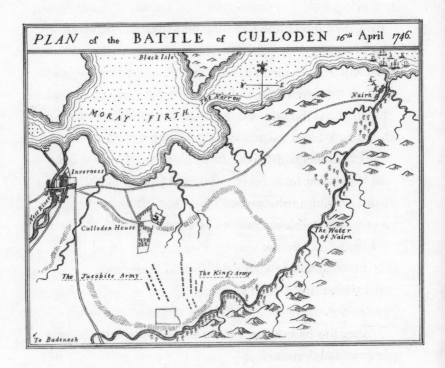

PLAN of the BATTLE of CULLODEN 16th April 1746.

L

I came to consciousness in a shiver. My body was shaking like a sapling in a gale. Blood fizzed and roared in my ears. My teeth bumped and rattled. Strange to say, I could feel my legs and feet although I was sure they were lying elsewhere. I thought I must shake to pieces. From a distance, I could hear the English sergeants muttering, over and over again: "Speed them on their way, men. They will thank you for it." And: "Despatch them, lads. Better than swinging in the yard of Carlisle gaol." Above me, in the way of a weak sun, was a horse and rider.

Hands tear at my coat and tunic. They brush aside the diamond and pull out my note-case. Letters and bank-notes flutter down. As if from another world, I hear a man speak.

"Sire, the officer has a commission from the King of France. He is prisoner-of-war."

"God damn the King of France! Do your duty, God damn you, Mr Harris!"

To be continued.